安三宝双喜制药厂
吴裕泰茶
家常菜
风格发廊
10:00-21:00
百事吉
McDonald's
SOVA
纤纤手
奔膻鲜酒楼
联想电脑专卖
太阳酒家
Budweiser
APEX
家常菜

跨世纪彩虹

艳俗艺术

策划人

廖雯　栗宪庭

艺术家

徐一晖
胡向东
俸振杰
王庆松
罗氏兄弟
刘峥
卢昊
张亚杰
邵振鹏
尹齐
孙平
李路明
赵勤　刘建
于伯公
刘力国
杨茂林（中国台湾）
顾世勇（中国台湾）
洪东禄（中国台湾）

1999

泰达当代艺术博物馆

湖南美术出版社

OUH, LA, LA, KITSCH!

Curators

Liao Wen   Li Xianting

Artists

Xu Yihui
Hu Xiangdong
Feng Zhenjie
Wang Qingsong
Luo Brother
Liu Zheng
Lu Hao
Zhang Yajie
Shao Zhenpen
Yin Qi
Sun Ping
Li Luming
Zhao Qin   Liu jian
Yu Bogong
Liu Liguo
Yang Maolin
Gu Shiyong
Hong Donglu

1999

TEDA Contemporary Art Museum

Hunan Fine Arts Publishing House

1 目录 Contents 1

生活在艳俗的汪洋大海

——艳俗艺术“反讽”的批判姿态

★ 廖雯

现在是公元1999年，20世纪最后的几个月。北京，中国的首都，中国的心脏，中国的窗口，当之无愧的中国当下文化和生存环境的样板模式：头戴琉璃瓦帽子、脚踩水泥底座、满身厕所瓷砖和蓝绿茶色玻璃的高大建筑毫无羞耻地站满繁华要道，满街的宾馆、商店、餐馆、洗浴洗足、美容美发、卡拉OK歌舞厅，也在一片声的水泥琉璃瓦、厕所瓷砖和蓝绿茶色玻璃中，以一串串彩旗彩球大红灯笼（晚上是一串串彩灯）、从天而降的招商标语、五彩缤纷的气球、别出心裁的塑胶吹气彩虹，争先恐后地争风露脸（即使我们从市里向郊外驰车几十公里，依然逃不过横叉在自然山水间的厕所瓷砖、蓝绿茶色玻璃、水泥“琉璃瓦”屋顶和胡涂乱抹的雕梁画栋）……满眼乱七八糟的俗艳，急功近利的暴发，满地打滚的廉价，没有根基的浮华。

这就是我们生活的“艳俗”的汪洋大海，这种文化在20世纪末的中国，已经泛滥成无法阻挡的“主流”文化。

新：半个世纪的浪漫理想

然而，这正是我们半个世纪以来，背弃古老文化建立新文化的浪漫“理想”。“新”即是这种浪漫理想的基本追求。

中国传统观念的“理想”看重的是子孙万代、流芳百世，而我们“理想”的目标是“打破一个旧世界，建立一个新中国”。因此古人崇尚自然法则，害怕因果报应，视“天人合一”为最高的境界，而我们注重人为能量，热衷现实成果，以“人定胜天”为始终的浪漫。

我们不妨还以“北京”为例。北京“自金代起，建都历史达700多年。有光荣的革命历史……解放前（1949年以前）是消费城市。解放后，钢铁、煤炭、石油化工、机械、电力、化学、纺织、造纸、印刷等工业迅速发展，已成为全国最大的综合性工业城市之一”(1)。把一个“历史达700多年”的古都，建设成“最大的综合性工业城市”，以及我们为这种理想具体描绘的高楼大厦，烟筒林立，电线飞扬的“动人”风景（这种风景充斥着我们50-80年代的宣传品），真的够理想，也真的够浪漫。

这种浪漫理想，鼓舞着成千上万的中国人，不断地拆旧盖新，其改天换地的速度，随著90年代商业文化的涌人更加迅猛。现在我们满眼望去，北京不仅作为古城的悠久历史荡然无存，甚至连50年代以来“新”中国的痕迹也时断时续，90年代的街景更是日新月异，北京成了永不完工的建筑工地。除了老城变新城，我们还创造了几年建立一座新城市的人类历史上的“奇迹”（如深圳），整个中国已经“旧貌变新颜”。我不知道人类是否都有“遗忘”的本能，即“人总是怀有某种愿望，想改写自己的经历，改变过去，抹掉他自己和别人的足迹”(2)，但“理想，同奋斗目标相联系的有实现可能性的想象”(3)，如今已经变成现实。

我们把“弘扬民族文化”和“实现现代化”的旗帜，抡成了大斧，打碎了古今中外所有价值、审美标准以及与这些标准密切相关的生活方式和艺术样式，转脸又用这些碎片拼凑起一个个自命

"现代化"的"新"的"奇迹"来。可惜，我们拥有"新"，拥有"奇迹"，拥有"强加给全人类的童年的理想"，但唯独不拥有现代性。

丑：整个中国的审美趣味

"新"不等于"现代"，从审美层面讲，是因为这种"新"并非由"现代"的审美价值体系所支撑。如我们的建筑毫

无节制地使用现代样式中的"直线"构成，以及水泥、钢管、玻璃等现代材料，而当我们把古代建筑中琉璃屋顶（甚至具装饰功能的斗拱、柱头、瓦当）的弧线，变成水泥（或金属）的直线直角的尖帽，把古塔木质的层层飞檐变成水泥（或瓷砖）的曲里拐弯的"狼牙棒"，拼在一座座直线风格的"大裤子、大肚子、大柱子"建筑之上时，我们不仅将西方现代直线风格的简洁、明朗、强调功能性等审美基础连跟拔起，而且也将中国古代的铺陈、优雅、注重装饰性的审美价值彻底毁灭。我们从满街的银行、邮局、餐馆、药店、甚至公共厕所，都作成如此畸形的红墙、琉璃瓦、雕梁画栋、石狮子、大红灯笼（或者古罗马宫殿的石膏雕像），都加上时髦、暴发的蓝绿茶色玻璃、金光闪闪的柱子、塑料片的门帘，到衣著、日用等日常生活中的一切，看到的都是这种在坍塌的审美价值碎片瓦砾中仓促间搭起的廉价、即时的布景。

对传统的断章取义，割断了文化的血脉，对现代的舍本逐末，又如同抽筋扒皮，我们打碎了古今中外所有的审美价值体系，"丑"即成了整个中国新的"审美趣味"。而且，这个无法代替的"丑"，不仅是一个美学判断，更是对我们日益失

去尊严的文化乃至道德境况作出的反映：那些充斥着媒体喋喋不休的相互吹捧，那些狂轰烂炸的广告中愚昧的笑容，那些出卖灵魂也自以为是的感动，那些巧夺天工的对自然的破坏欲……

把如此"丑"的艳俗称为"审美趣味"，是因为其一，这种趣味由于植根于前面所说的"浪漫理想"，先天具有与大众打成一片（为工农兵喜闻乐见）的"抒情性"。正是这点"酸"，在很大程度上诱发了人们对"美好"的梦想，所以，艳俗虽"丑"却快乐喜庆。其二，我不知道还有多少人面对这种"人文风景（是否称人"瘟"风景更妥）"还能感觉到"丑"，人们是否已经在这种环境中生活得异常快乐，遗忘了对审美享乐的渴望，丧失了对审美享乐的能力，因为当一种现象变得普遍、平凡、无所不在时，就不再被关注了，因为武功再好也难敌千军万马铺天盖地而来，更因为这种"丑"的势无阻挡的泛滥和流行，向我们描述了一种无法回避的真实，甚至一种过剩的力量。

绝望喜剧——艳俗艺术"反讽"的批判姿态

作为自命对当下文化负有责任的当代艺术家，生活在艳俗的汪洋大海而无能为力，使我们常常陷于哭笑不得的尴尬境地。我不知道艺术是否可以警世可以改变社会，但我们至少可以揭示这样一种生存现实，使我们在面对它的时候，能够始终保持不同流合污的独立的批判立场，这即是艳俗艺术的奢望。

艳俗艺术于1990年代中期兴起⑷。1996年5月，《大众样板》、《艳妆生活》，及相继的《浮华的伤害》、《皮肤的叙述》⑸等艳俗艺术的展览，集中导致了一个艺术热点，其学术观点我们也已经在

当时和其后的诸篇文章⑹中深入细致地阐述过。当时，我们把握了“艳俗”作为当下文化的重要的针对点，艺术家采用的“反讽（过分模拟艳俗的某种特征以达到嘲讽效果）”⑺的批判姿态也基本一致和清晰，但作品存在的问题也是显而易见的。其一，语言的近亲繁殖：萝卜、白菜、鲜花、美女等符号，几乎是每个艺术家作品的首选，夸张、平涂、光亮的广告手法也基本雷同。其二，语言不到位：模仿停留在艳俗的样式上，看上去与现实的艳俗区别不大，反讽的效果自然大打折扣。

这之后的三年间，坚守的艳俗艺术家（一部分原来的艳俗艺术家转向关注其他问题），以及不断出现的关注艳俗的新的艺术家，继续努力工作，于是我们这个展览就拥有了一批新的作品和新的展示意义。这些新作品与以往作品相比，都更加智慧地使用了中国俗文化中约定俗成的行为方式，充分发挥了民间工艺制作方法的特长，不同程度地完善了个性化的语言方式即个人触点。

徐一晖的《艺术屎》巧妙地利用中文“艺术史”和“艺术屎”的同音不同义，并模拟中国民间的供奉方式，把这泡叮着苍蝇的“艺术屎”，用俗艳的花朵和雕琢的“奖杯”，供在本该供菩萨供财神的地方，而黄色的屎被涂成黄金色，也就染上了发财的梦想；周围是模拟的中国民间的花字⑻楹联：横批是“艺术屎”，两边对联的“文艺一枝花，全靠它当家”，套用的是50年代著名的“庄稼一枝花，全靠肥当家”的流行口号，这一置换又巧妙地利用了“屎”与“肥”的同义不同字，艺术史在严肃与可笑、严谨与虚华、高尚与低俗、创造与赚钱之间变得模棱两可，表达出他对艺术

日益丧失尊严的无奈，艺术自身媚俗问题的反省，以及对艺术和艺术史的根本质疑。《金钱》则利用中文“金钱”的词同义不同，即“可以消费的真钱”与“金色的作为摆设的假钱”，以及中国民间常见的祈求梦想（许愿）的方式（如以金元宝祈财，以布娃娃祈子，以五谷祈丰收，以龙牌位祈雨，以福禄寿诸神祈荣华富贵等），揭示出人们对“发财”的梦想及其虚幻的实质。徐一晖是最早直接使用民间工艺制作方式的艺术家，他现在已经可以驾轻就熟地发挥陶瓷工艺的特长，完善个人的语言方式，如奖杯浮雕的雕琢、瓷花字的繁琐、屎与钱黄金色的暴发，都恰到好处地加强了作品的反讽力度。

胡向东的《理想种植》种下的一棵棵“水晶白菜”，让人想起民间传说中贪婪的种金子、种玉的故事。他本来想直接用民间工艺作为摆设的雕刻的“玉白菜”（也有用象玉质的石头仿制的廉价的“假玉白菜”），但“玉白菜”虽然也有炫耀富贵的暴发意味，但造价昂贵。几经实验，最终选择了接近“玉”质的树脂，自然材料换成工业材料，精雕细刻换成小批量生产的简陋的民间铸模工艺，并且做得比真白菜还大（玉白菜只有真白菜的一半大），树脂半透明的假玉质感，铸模工艺的假雕刻感觉，把农民式暴发梦想的虚华揭示得无以附加。而把这虚华的梦想种到地里暗含的对“收获”的祈望，就如同等待煮熟的鸡蛋孵出小鸡一般令人啼笑皆非了。

俸振杰的《幸福》和《浪漫旅程》系列作品，以流行的“婚纱摄影”为蓝本，准确地把握了人们对“幸福感”和“浪漫情调”的本能向往，被滥用、贱卖就会变成“媚俗需要”这一契入点，

揭示出媚俗不仅仅是一种艳俗的样式，而“存在一种媚俗的趣味，媚俗的行为，媚俗的人对媚俗的需要：凝视美化谎言镜子的需要，被镜子中自己的影像感动流下喜悦的眼泪的需要”⑼。他是少数依然保持绘画方式的艳俗艺术家，而新郎新娘幸福得发紫的脸和变形的笑容，“世界公园”⑽小人国、游乐园式的背景，以及借鉴月份牌年画光亮的处理方法，不仅体现出鲜明的个人感觉方式，也已经脱离了传统油画技法的巢臼。

卢昊的《花》、《鸟》、《鱼》、《虫》，让中国人著名的畸形消闲物——花鸟鱼虫，住进作为北京城市象征的著名建筑模型，做成了更为畸形的人民大会堂花盆，美术馆鸟笼、天安门鱼缸、新华门虫罐，提示出我们生活的城市环境已经与自然环境层层隔绝。一方面，“花鸟鱼虫”作为市民消闲消费物，从开始就被畸形化，已经在很大程度上与其自然本性隔了一层；另一方面，被市民当作自然消遣的玩“花鸟鱼虫”的享乐，也是文化畸形的产物，与享乐自然又隔了一层。有机玻璃透明但隔膜的特性，准确地体现出这种似是而非的多重隔膜感。

张亚杰的《典型》准确地把握了中国“光荣榜”式的“典型形象”。这些被统一规范的样板，从少先队标兵，到各行各业的模范，不仅具有统一的行为标准，而且具有统一的形象特征，以及统一的媚俗表情：随和、喜庆、不显露个性。张亚杰使用民间镶嵌假眼、程式化的塑造方式，使这些“典型”有一种共同的亦真亦假、似亲犹隔的感觉，揭示人们生活在被规划统一模式中的可悲和可笑。

王庆松的《思想者》、《拿来千佛手》，使用自我扮演和电脑拼接的方法，模拟佛教信徒虔诚的打坐、祈祷姿态和表情，却是胸前刻着麦当劳，手里拿著各种名牌产品，这种对名牌的宗教般的“崇拜”，揭示出消费文化对人们生活冲击，已经侵蚀到了灵魂。只穿内裤和白菜、垃圾桶底座的的亵渎、滑稽，电脑喷绘在丝绒、绸缎上的光亮，都给这种崇拜增添了农民气息。

罗氏兄弟的《欢迎世界名牌》集合、拼接了中国各个时期的宣传符号，从“恭喜发财”、“年年有余”、“吉祥如意”的年画，到当下流行的商品广告，统统笼罩在光芒四射的光圈中，表明人们对以“世界名牌”为标志的消费文化的崇拜，已经蔚然成风，且势不可挡。罗氏兄弟也是较早使用民间工艺的艳俗艺术家，他们将传统漆画工艺的鲜艳、光亮发挥到极致，加强了这种崇拜的浮华气氛和暴发色彩。

刘峥的《仿月份牌》、《庐山恋》、《时髦女郎》，在中国半个世纪流行的结婚送礼的尼龙绸缎被面上绣满了亮晶晶的珠花，连接起中国半个多世纪的流行美女——20—40年代的月份牌美女、70—80年代爱情电影中的美女、90年代的时髦女郎同样艳俗特征：漂亮、造作而无思想。

邵振鹏的《中国制造》采用仿红木的家具制造工艺，将同是“中国制造”的传统的椅子造型、革命时代的红旗五星、葵花麦穗、青松翠柏图案，与当下流行的美女形象融会在一起，“中国制造”不仅是中国由古代传统、革命传统向消费时代过渡象征，而且是中国逐步成为西方商品加工场的标志。

于伯公的《长满毛发的大便》、《满怀理想的大便》，用皇帝专用的金黄色绸缎和民间布制工艺

缝制的“大便”，软绵绵、暄腾腾，或披著时髦女人装饰纱似的毛发，或生长出粉红色的翅膀，看似金光灿烂、理想浪漫，实质滑稽可笑、令人作呕，连叮在上面的苍蝇都戴上了防毒面具，嘲讽了中国艳俗文化以恶俗为高雅的有钱而无知的心态。

刘力国的《经典》以民间陶瓷繁复、雕琢的制作工艺，将俗文化中祈求荣华富贵的“经典”语符如龙凤呈祥、祥云仙鹤、荷花蟠桃、鲜花金钱等吉祥物，与被视为低级趣味的屁股堆砌在一起，表达出对当下暴发式的假高贵、伪豪华的蔑视。

李路明的《中国手姿》把中国佛像文化的典型手姿作了色情化、流行化的处理，于是手姿本来的优雅、高贵、神秘，变成了类似流行美女的手姿的矫饰、造作、俗气；并以捧圣物的类似的姿态捧着同样性感、时髦、廉价的高跟鞋等流行物品，揭示出中国当下变高雅为恶俗的农民式的俗文化情境。

孙平的《时尚文化小姐》、《为您服务小姐》、《前卫艺术小姐》，选择了“小姐”这个消费文化中的经典语符，并直接使用与此相关的现成品——服装模特和不干胶的流行话语“天天好梦”、“无限享受”、“为您服务”、“潇洒走一回”、“恭喜发财”、“loveyou”、“Happy”等等，于是随著“小姐”的广泛流通，消费文化污染了从市井社会到艺术领域的每一个角落，已经成为不可逆转的事实。

赵勤和刘建的《我爱麦当劳》、《现场直播》对“一家人吃麦当劳”和“媒体现成直播”的选择，准确地把握了当下流行文化中最时髦、最泛滥也最媚俗的情境；在同一个标准场景、标准姿态上，随意画画，即繁衍出无数类似的场景：尽管名目、地点、身份、性别、年龄各异，但无论农村城市、中国外国，无论工农学商、男女老幼，几乎是一个模子克隆出来的统一模式，而且大家在这种统一模式中个个欢天喜地，这种奇特的处理方式，有趣地反讽了流行文化赶时髦、随大流的媚俗心态和统一生活模式的泛滥，并显示出年轻一代（70年代以后出生）艺术家特有的轻松的调侃心态。

尹齐旅居法国多年，近年来又大量的时间留在中国，他看中国艳俗有完全不同的感受。他精心选择了一些很小的艳俗工艺品，如亮晶晶的蝴蝶发卡，粉气的塑料房子，表情奇怪（尹齐说有点恶）的自由女神像，用广告式的美化手法，把这些价格和感觉都“便宜”的工艺品拍得精致、漂亮，而这些工艺品放大到一定程度呈现的奇妙的失真感，正是被法国轻松浪漫审美情调熏陶过的尹齐，为中国艳俗文化制造的超现实的神话色彩。

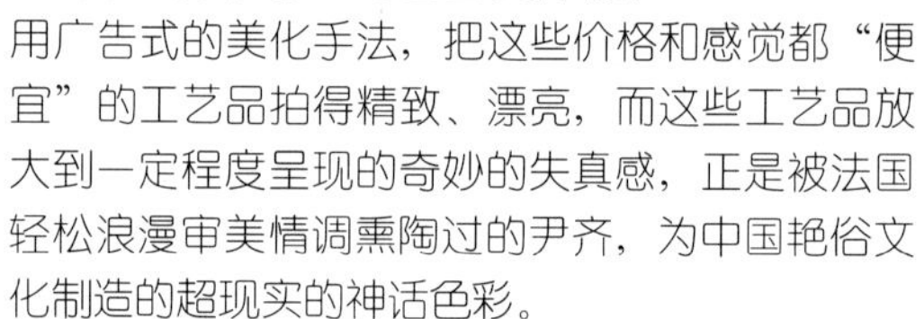

此展览还特邀了三位中国台湾艺术家：杨茂林、顾世勇、洪东禄。

因为，“在当今中国台湾的生活视觉中，从电动玩具到电子媒体的广告讯息；从婚俗喜事、传统节庆、各级选举，一直到用酷哥辣妹以广招徕的休闲生活等等全面活动；艳色妆扮得煽情火热，而且瞬息快速在流行浪涛中变换的现象，已经成为庶民生活尤其是年轻新生代习以常见的主流”，但有趣的是，与中国大陆艳俗艺术家自觉的批判立场相比，中国台湾的艳俗对于艺术家而言，“只是他们为达各自目的，借道而行的途径之一”(11)。我们从这三位中国台湾艺术家的作品中可窥一斑。

杨茂林始终关注文化问题，其作品使用的语

符与中国台湾每个历史时期的流行文化密切相关，因此，90年代这批作品带有“艳俗”倾向（90年代中国台湾流行文化的主要趣味）实属顺理成章。日本卡通、美国机器人，流行的性娱乐工具，以及民俗的剪纸、对联、胡萝卜等，共同构成中国台湾当下文化主流，也共同辩证着中国台湾文化的整合与再生。

顾世勇的《2001年1月1日—回家的路上》，以不名飞行物作为梦想更“完满”生活的引导，并“试图打造一个新神话”⑿，而穿着中国红棉袄、抱着象征不明飞行物金球的女孩，穿梭在现实的大街小巷，营造出的“天真浪漫的喜庆仪式”⒀，则昭示出这种梦想的世俗根基。

洪东禄作为中国台湾更年轻一代的艺术家，对流行文化的感受和把握更为简单而直接。《龙来了》、《春丽》等，将流行的美国芭比娃娃、日本美少女、假面机器人等塑料卡通玩偶，或放置在西方古老传统文化的背景如教堂，西方现代的街景,或与负载着中国古老概念的现代工艺“龙”拼接在一起，跨越人类时空的文化，即在这种直接的组合中模糊了距离，并共同演示着跨世纪的文化神话。

啊！艳俗艺术真似一出喜剧：热闹、喜庆、幽默，且始终以类似喜剧的批判姿态—反讽，揭示着我们生活中人们习以为常的荒诞的一面。

大家熟悉的电视剧《编辑部的故事》、《我爱我家》，今年春节联欢晚会唯一可看的小品《实话实说》等，与艳俗艺术的这种批判姿态异曲同工。然而，“我们越是长久而细致地欣赏一则玩笑故事，就越是感到悲哀”⒁。从这个角度而言，艳俗艺术无异于一出绝望喜剧。

1999年3—4月

注：

⑴《辞海》（1979年上海辞书出版社）“北京市”条。

⑵米兰·昆德拉（Milan Kundera）《六十三个词》“遗忘”条。

⑶《辞海》（1979年上海辞书出版社）“理想”条。

⑷见栗宪庭《有关艳俗艺术成因的补遗》。

⑸1996年，栗宪庭、廖雯在北京策划的两个艳俗艺术的专题展览和相继的两个艳俗艺术的个人展览。

⑹⑺见栗宪庭的《波普之后：艳俗话语与反讽模仿》、《对“农民式的暴发趣味”的仿讽—中国艳俗艺术语境述评续补》（附录）、廖雯《平民时代的贵族布景 —— “艳俗”的文化品位和艺术品质》。

⑻以花朵组字，也有以花鸟、人物组字的，或画或绣，用于祝寿等喜庆场合。

⑼米兰·昆德拉《六十三个词》“媚俗”条。

⑽按比例模拟缩小的世界名胜古迹的游乐公园。

⑾胡永芬《台湾艳俗 —— 生活是如此妆扮》。

⑿⒀顾世勇的《2001年1月1日—回家的路上》。

⒁米兰.昆德拉《六十三个词》“笑”条。

Living in Kitsch

—The critical sarcasm of Gaudy Art

★ Liao Wen

The time is 1999, a few months away from the end of the 20th Century.The place is Beijing, China's Capital, heart of the nation, window to the outside world. As a perfect example of modern life and culture, this is what meets the eye: City blocks filled with concrete buildings, capped with a pseudo glazed rooftop, covered by bathroom tiles and tinted glasses windows. Squeezed in between then are small guesthouses, restaurants, bathhouses, hair saloons and karaok bars air, screaming for clients using lanterns and christmas lights in all seasons, banners, balloons and even inflated plastic rainbows. (Even if we drive miles into the countryside, we can find the same buildings splashed across a natural landscape). Our eyes are assaulted by the chaotic world of kitsch. We are surrounded by instant millionaires with cheap products an affluence without foundation.

We are submerged in kitsch, the unstoppable mainstream Chinese culture at of the end of the Century.

The New:A Chinese Romance for the Latter Half of the Century

The "Romance of the New" is a dream that has been pursued by the Chinese for the past 50 years. To do away with antiquity, to build "new" things to forget about tradition, let's "destroy the old world and build a new China". Our forefathers worshipped nature, prayed for celestial and earthly harmony.They feared nature forceful revenge . Today, we believe in manpower, practical achievements, we want to prove we can "conquer the sky".

Beijing is a perfect example of this pursuit of the New. The City was built 700 years ago in the Jing Dynasty. Uptill 1949, it was a center of gentile consumption. After the revolution, Beijing became an industrial center for iron, steel, coal, petrochemical, machinery, textile, printing, etc".[1] With amazing speed, a 700 year old capital was transformed into an industrial hub. Beijing's skyline is one of puffing chiminies and crisscrossing electric wires. This same scenery has been the subject of theme posters from 1950s to 1980s.

The "Romance of the New" has inspired the Chinese to dismantle the past. The commercial culture the 1990s has escalated the ferocity of this destruction. Antiquity has vanished, even the "old" new of the 1950's is being taken down at great speed. The Beijing of the 1990's is a permanent construction site. We are not only in the business of transforming the old, we also want to micaculously something entirely "new". I am not sure whether man has the ability to forget that "man has harboured a desire to edit one's own records, to change the past, to erase traces of relationship".[2] But what I do know is " that idealism which is fused with goals and the possibility of realization"[3] has become reality.

The chinese bulldozer has swept accross the nation under the banners of "modernization" and "ethnic culture". It has cleared away all remanents of previously established social value systems and esthetic standard, along with them, a lifestyle and art form also bit the dust. What appeared afterwards, was a self-professed "new, miraculous modernization". Which rose from the debris, to claim and reinforce the Romance of the New to our children.Unfortunately,all this "newness", "miracle" and "modernization" is not what is needed for a "modern civilization".

The Ugly: Chinese esthetics

"New" can not be modern unless supported by an esthetic value system. If we build with a modern straight line, but add to it curves of antiquity, if we allow oursevles to replace the gentle sloping of a classic wooden roof with plates of hard concret, if we imitate the graceful arch of glazed tiles with bent metals, we are destrying esthetic values. For, we have uprooted the simplicity, the straight fowardness and the functionlism of the straight line, and at the same time, distortedly plagerized the sumptuousness, elegance classical Chinese architecture, misinterpreting the emphasis on the decorative. Whether it is a bank or a public toilet, any public building in China is most likely to have a pseudo red wall, fake glazed tiles, or stone lions, red lanerns (perhaps even some Roman images as well). These features are unforgivingly combined with green or blue shaded glass, shiny copper plated columns and aluminium window frames. It is a cheap scenery built on the bankruptcy of an esthetic system, and built in hast.

To plagerize tradition, to interrupt cultural continuity, to copy without understanding are habits which inevitably lead to the new esthetic of ugliness. The "New Ugliness" is not only an esthetic judgement, it is a testement to the delapidated state of moral standards and human dignity. This is the age in which media indulges in mutual flattery, the age of the advertisement with the same stupid smile in every form; the age when Faust becomes a moral role model for the young, and the desire to reshape nature is handed such an awsome tool……

There are two reasons why the Ugliness of kitsch can be termed an esthetic interest. First, the interest is a result of the pursuit of the New, the "Romance of the New" is a popular movement. It is very cliched and appleals to the masses. To a large extent, it stirs up dreams of a "good", kitsch is ugly, but merry. Secondly, I am not sure how many people can still detect the ugliness. It could be that everyone is living happily in this environment. People have forgotten the desire to admire beauty and lost the ability to enjoy it. For when a phenomena becomes phenomenal, it ceases to an issue. However well trained, a one man show cannot outwit the onslaught of millions. The ugliness is irresistable, it describes an unavoidable reality. It is all powerful.

Desperate Comedy: the Sarcasm of Gaudy Art

For an artist who lives and breaths in kitsch, but still feels some responsibility towards culture, the situation is at best awkward. I do not want to argue that art can change society, but at least art can disclose a reality so as to remind all of us to be critical and independent of our environment. This is the aspiration of Gaudy Art.

Gaudy Art in C.hina was born in the mid 1990s. In May, 1996, there was a flurry of Gaudy Art exhibitions: Popular Model, the Gaudy Life and Damaged by Affluence. Critics including myself have already written about the academic value in great detail. At the time, I was of the opinion that Guady Art is a direct reflection of the current culture. The sarcasm is clearly expressed through an exaggerated imitation of kitsch. But problems remained in the art works: Firstly, the vocabulary is repeatitive, symbols such as cabbages, flowers and girls keep reappearing in different works. Even the technique, a flat shinny surface and advertisement style brushstrokes, are also similar among different artists. Secondly, Gaudy Art is too close to kitsch, the question of "is it real or is it memorax" does arise. When Guady Art's own vocabulary is underdeveloped and yet it tries to exagerate kitsch, it is potentially damaging to the implied sarcasm in the art work.

Today, three years after Gaudy art first appeared, our exhibition is replenished by new works and a new concept is presented by artists who continued to explore Gaudy Art. (Some artists left the group to find other forms of expressions) and others joined rank.

In comparision with the works presented three years ago, these works show different levels of maturity, presenting a more personal perspective and vocabulary. These works intelligently borrowed aspects of the kitsch format, and demonstrated the artists talent in using technique in chinese folk art.

"Yishushi", by Xu Yi-hui cleverly used the synonym "Shi" , the former means history and the latter,shit. Hence "Yishushi" can mean either art history or artistic shit. Xu uses colorful flowers and heavily decorated trophy to elevate this fly catching "shit" on the altar piece. His use of gold in the "shit" hints at dream of fabulous wealth. Surrounding the altar are classical Chinese triplets, which are usually used to docorate doorways in rural China. The horizontal reads "art shit". The two vertical stanza read "Art is a flower, Master of the home". This is a further pun or a popular slogan in stanza from the fifties. The original two stanza were "Grain is a flower, Fertilizer is the Master". Again, Xu points fun, exchanging "shit" for and "fertilizer". Xu's work is both serious and humorous, maticulous and superficial, elegant and grotesque, creative and gready. "Yishushi" is an expression of the artist's helplessness in face of an art which is becoming base; it is his own reflection on art becoming kitsch, as well as his serious doubts on the value system for art and art history today. Jinqian, is another pun. It means literally "gold money" but also infers means "wealth" in Chinese. Gold Money, which is used only for decorative and symbolic purposes, is often burned in folk ceremonies to pray for wealth. (the Chinese would also make dolls to pray for as baby, grain to pray for a good harvest, the dragon for rain, etc.). Jinqian reveals the illusion of wealth as well as the desire and need for the illusion. Xu Yihui is one of the earliest artists to use folk art techniques. He has now perfected his skills in porcelain as well as his personal vocabulary. The relief on the trophy with complicated procelain letters and explosion of gold "shit" and gold money ,perfectly expresses the strength of the author in his use of sarcasm.

"Dream Plants" by Hu Xiang-dong includes "Crystal Cabbages".The work evokes the folk tale about the greedy man who plants seed hoping to grow gold and jade. Hu originaliy wanted to use traditional craft techniques to make sculptures called "Jade Cabbages" as well as use cheap fake Jade to mak "Imitation Jade Cabbages". But jade cabbages are symbolic of overnight wealth but alas are, too expensive to be made. After several experiments, he chose resin as material, as this is close to jade in appearance. As the work evolved, natural material was replaced by industrial material, delicate carving was replaced by simple molding, miniture jade objects were replaced by larger-than-life cabbages. The final work and its evolution is an accurate statement of the desire for wealth in Chinese peasantry. Planted in the ground.The resin cabbage takes on additional level of sarcasm posing as the symbol and dream of a good harvest.

"Happiness" and "Romantic Journey" by Feng Zheng-jie are a series of works that thematically use Chinese wedding photos as their subject. Feng's criticism points at the commercial manipulation of the desire to feel good and romantic, which has greatly cheapened the human pursuit of happiness. Feng's work reveals to us that kitsch is not merely a form, but also a matter of taste and a behavior pattern. Kitschmensch need kitsch, "the compulsion to stare into a mirror which lies about reality, so much so that one sheds tears of joy upon seeing ones reflection".[4] Feng is the only painter among the Gaudy artists. His figures wear a visage of happiness that is more than blush, it is almost purple. In the background, hovers images of amusement parks and other popular leisure destinations. The surface of his paintings have the smoothness and brightness of a calender poster. Through this combination together, Feng has arrived at a personal style with a technique that comes from but also escapes the clichÈ of traditional paintings.

Flowers, Birds, Fish and Bugs are four popular playthings for Mandarin Chinese who mostly live in the city of Beijing. Lu Hao has removed these playthings from their usual cages and put them into symbols of Beijing's architecture. The Great Hall of the People is a vase, the National Art Gallery is a bird cage, Tianamen is a fishtank and Xinhua Men is a bug jar. This dislocation illustrates the separation of city life and nature. On the one hand, the fact that natural objects have become playthings is itself a distortion of nature, it takes nature out of nature. On the other hand, these distorted playthings are admired by city dwellers, which further separates the people from nature. Plexiglass is a perfect material to express such a state of solid separation,but apparent transparency.

"Models" by Zhang Ya-jie has a firm grip on the concept of the role model in Chinese society. These Models of conformity, from Little Pioneers to model works, are not only measured by their behavior but are also required to look the same. They must display the same attitude: easy going, happy-go-lucky pleasing with no trace of personality. Zhang used tradition method for the doll's eyes and plastic extrusions to create that sameness, a uniformity that is sad and comical at the same time.

Wang Qing-song posed himself in his works, the images were treated on computer. In Thinker and Thousand Hand Budhar, the author mimicked meditation positions with a visage of sincerity. Yet, on his chest is carved McDonalds and in his hands are luxury brand items. This is a clear statement that consumerism, along with fashion, are not only social diseases but have also contaminated the soul. The peasant flavor of Wang's work is fully realized in the image of a man in his underpants with his cabbages and garbage heap and the computer spray painted onto velvet and brocade.

In the works of the Luo Brothers, the artists are telling us that we have been bought and conquered by name brands. In Welcome World Famous Brands, popular holiday greetings such as "Get Rich", "Have Extra" and "Happiness be with You" are grouped together with commerical goods under a huge ray of light. The Luo Brothers were also the earliest artists to experiment with folk art techniques. Their works are lacqure paintings, a form of craftswork in China. Its characteristic is brilliant color and shine. This technique lends itself to the artist's statements on an atmosphere of affluence and the smell of the nouveau riche.

Like A Calender, Love of Lushan and Fashion Girl are works by Liu Zheng. The brocade quilt cover has been a tradtional gift at chinese weddings for half a century. Liu has embrodered beeds on the covers, together with canlender girls from the 1920s to the 1940s, movie starlets from the 1970s and 1980s and super model from the 1990s. The work is a reflection of a state of mind: pretty things, loud things, empty things.

Shao Zhen-peng imitates classical Chinese Rosewood furniture in his work,"Made In China".He has fused classical shape of the chair with revolutionary red flags and stars, sunflowers and pines, as well as beauty queens. "Made in China" is not only a statement of how China developed from traditional society to revolution ary society and finally to a consumer market economy, It is also trying to say that China has at last become a source of cheap commercial goods to be sold in the West.

"Shit with Long Hair", "Shit with a Dream" are works by Yu Bo-gong. He used gold colored brocade which was reserved for the clothing of the emporor, to saw piles of soft and gregarious "shit". He has also given them hair like a woman's veil and pink cushy wings. His work is ridiculously funny and disgusting, even the fly is wearing a mask. The author is laughing at the nouveau riche, for whom money can easily substitute elegance and intellect.

Classics is a denounciation of the new cultural hypocrites and their pretention of having class. Liu Li-guo uses a folk technique in procelain making carving and reliefs to depict kitsch symbols of prestige such as dragons, phoenix, cranes and lotus blossom combined with base images of buttocks.

Li Lu-ming's work "Chinese Hand Gestures" is a play on Buddhist hand postures. He has distorted the sacred positions making them erotic and common. What was previously a symbol of elegance and mystery is transformed into the fashionable gestures of starlets. Not only has he degraded the gestures, he has also put into these hands kistch objects such as high heeled shoes. Li's work shows his total disgust at the distortion of what is sacred to be base and commercial.

As "Miss" becomes a popular and overused title for a woman in a market economy China, (in all corners of urban China, one can hear someone calling "miss"!, a sure sign of overdeveloped commercial culture). Sunping has chosen this word to represent his works: "Miss Fashion", "Miss Service", and "Miss Advant Guard". He has also used objects directly associated with "Miss", fashion garment and accessories, as well as those over sweet greetings such as "at your service", "endless enjoyment", "have a nice dream", "live it up", and I love you, etc.

"I love McDonalds" and "Live Broadcast" has completely captured the most outstanding symbol of kitsch. The repetition of the same family eating hamburgers or in a supermarket style broadcast program emphasizes the pervasiveness of such cultural trends. The author, Zhao Qin and Liu Jian has repainted the same scene with people from all walks of life, peasants, students, businessman, male, female, old and young and cloned them into the same ecstatic expression. The authors humorously ridicule the "go with the flow" mentality and give a serious subject a sense of lightness (a **phenomoman** is unique to artists born in the 1970s).

Although Yin Qi has spent the last few years in China, his residence in France has given him a different perspective on kitsch. Yin has carefully photographed a selection of small kitsch objects, such as bright butterfly hairpins, pink plastic houses. The statue of Liberty with a strange expression. (Yin says it is a look of disgust). The photos were shot like advertisements, which beautify the objects to the maximum. The effect is such that these small objects are blown up out of proportion and so loose all sense of reality. Yin's work glorifies small kitsch objects, and to certain extent demonstrate a French romantic humour.

The Exhibition has also invited three Taiwanese artists: Yang Mao-ling, Gu Shi-yong and Hong Dong-lu.

"A major diffference between Taiwanese and mainland Gaudy Artists is that gaudy art is only a method to express their subject matter, it is a borrowed premises".[5] Again the reason that Gaudy Art becomes an important premises is because in Taiwan, mainstream culture, especially for the young is mainly made up of electronic toys, interactive computers and advertisements. Even at weddings, holidays and elections, vocabulary such as "cool brother" and "hot sister" is part of everyday life.

Yang Mao-lin's subject has always been the state of culture. His vocabulary is closely affiliated with cultural symbols in Taiwan from different historical periods. His work in the 1990's has a gaudy flavor which is totally logical considering the cultural background of the time. Japanese cartoons, American Robots, fun sex aids and Cshinese folk paper cuts, caligraphy and carrots combine to give structural impression of current culture in Taiwan.

"On the Road home - January 1st, 2001" by Gu Shi-yong uses UFO as the harbinger of dreams, it is an attempt to create new dreams. The image of a girl in a traditional Chinese outfit holding a golden UFO wondering down streeets is one that is based on the kitsch dream, which creates a sense of innocent uforia.

Hong Dong-lu is an artist of the younger generation. His understanding of popular culture is simpler and more direct. He uses Barbie dolls, Japanese teenagers, masks, robots and other plastic toys in a traditional background of churches or modern streets to merge the old and the new but also to emphasize the felt but not spoken distance between now and then.

Wow! Gaudy art is a comedy: lively, happy, humourous, but like all good comedies it pocesses the sense of sarcasm. It reads the senseless side of our existance. What we see on televison, comedies such as Story of an Editorial Office, I love my home, and even the talk show Be honest is successful for the same reason.

As for all good comedies, at some point a sense of sadness creeps in. "Gaudy Art" is no different, it is a desperate comedy for the end of the Century.

Notes

1"Beijing", Encyclopedia, Shanghai Encyclopedia Publishing House, 1979.

2 "Forgeting" ,Sixty-three Words, by Milan Kundera.

3 "Romance" Encyclopedia, Shanghai Encyclopedia Publishing House, 1979.

4 "Kitsch" ,Sixty-three Words, by Milan Kundera.

5 Boorish and Vulgar as the Makeup of Life, by Hu Yong-fen.

(translater: Hong Huang Proofing: Lucy England)

有关“艳俗艺术”成因的补遗

★ 栗宪庭

其实，我在前两篇文字中已经提过，艳俗术艺一是受过JEFF KOONS的影响。因为中国当代艺术的20年，其中一些潮流多与输人的资讯有关，80年代，JEFF KOONS在西方曾红极一时，80年代末和90年代初，国内当代艺术的圈子，就开始流传JEFF KOONS的画册。二是它直接导源于政治波普和玩世写实主义的形式因素和创作态度，所谓形式因素，即指在色彩和选材上的艳俗倾向，如1990年，曾涉足政治波普的张培力，画过“健美”系列，选材和色彩都很艳俗。玩世写实主义的代表艺术家方力钧、宋永红，其1992年的作品，画面色彩也非常艳俗。尤其政治波普晚出的艺术家祁志龙，1992年他初涉波普时，一出手就是艳星美女大花朵，除了作品中的政治因素，几近于后来的艳俗，或者说祁志龙可以算作艳俗艺术的先导艺术家之一，这是我后来把祁志龙的作品也归人艳俗艺术的原因，而且祁志龙那时就把自己的作品命名为“消费形象”。这就是我说的在“创作态度”上，政治波普对艳俗艺术的启发，即政治波普表达的是“西方消费文化对社会主义政治意识形态冲击”所造成的心理感觉，而玩世写实主义也表达的是一种日常、平庸的生活姿态和感觉。当然，政治波普和玩世是一种转换的姿态，即玩世的泼皮，以及政治波普中用消费形象调侃政治形象，这个潮流在表达逃离政治的心态时，所必然包含的几分政治含义。而在这种转换的过程中，如果把王广义的《大批判》和余友涵的《毛和惠特尼》这种典型政治波普的作品，与晚出的祁志龙的艳星美女大花朵作比较，祁志龙作品中的政治形象已经减弱，而消费形象开始突出出来，这一点非常重要，这是我把政治波普、玩世中有艳俗倾向，和艳俗艺术本身作区别的关键点。因为艳俗艺术的批评定位，不是转折——借助消费文化和平庸的生活从政治中逃离的心态，而是消费文化已经在中国大行其事后的种种艳俗的现实感觉，或者说，艳俗艺术是艺术家直觉到在西方消费文化被引进中国后，所召唤或沉滓泛起的是一种农民式的暴发理想和现实，这并不是现代消费文化本身，因为现代消费文化依赖的是一个全面现代化的社会和价值标准的基础，而中国还没有这个基础。

30年代月份牌年画

清末工艺油画

至于为什么说艳俗艺术的文化针对性是“借助西方消费文化，召唤或沉滓泛起的农民式暴发趣味和现实。”我以为任何文化，都是以一定的价值系统支撑的样式体系，而近百年，我们在与传统文化决裂之后，又在接受西方文化的冲击中，没有真正接受西方文化的价值系统，从“中体西用”，到“中体”变为社会主义的意识形态，其中支撑我们文化的，只是注重短期效用的政治功利主义，这种价值标准，就不可能建设一个相对恒定的文化样式系统，所谓传统文化，所谓西方文化，对于今天的现实空间，就只是一种以功利主义的态度，随不同的使用目的，而随意摘取的文化样式中的碎片。我不知道这还能否称其为文化，姑且称之为“习性文化”，即在中国这样一个社会结构里，权力结构中人是依照个人习性中“残留的记忆”和“即兴的需求”来选取“文化”的，文化对于这种个人，必然是一种无系统的碎片状态，而权力中人的农民成分（参

安迪·沃

董希文·开国大典

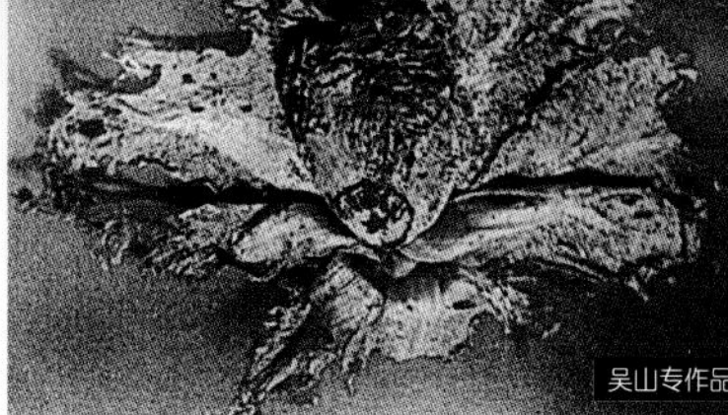
吴山专作品

看拙文《对农民暴发趣味的仿讽》)，自然会把现代消费文化变成一种“恭喜发财、8888、大红灯笼”之类的东西。当然，关于“习性文化”的说法肯定太简单，只有留待以后探讨。

正是从消费文化的表面意义上，中国的艳俗艺术在语言上受到了JEFF KOONS的影响，这很自然，任何艺术家都是在一定的语言传统和线索上工作的，重要的是这些艺术家的感觉，是否来源于我们今天这个艳俗的现实，以及他们怎样来表达他们对这个现实的感觉，或者说他们在接受JEFF KOONS的影响时，怎样转换为自己的语言方式，这是我们关注的重点。

皮艾尔、吉尔斯作品

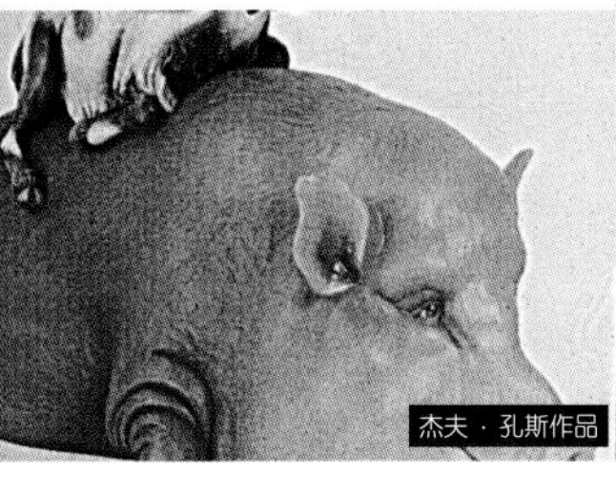
杰夫·孔斯作品

前面提到，从政治波普向艳俗艺术的转换上，祁志龙很重要。而我格外推崇的是徐一晖。徐一晖是‘85新潮中的人物，之后他无所事事多年，1991—1992年，我正在策划《后‘89中国新艺术展》和《MAO GOES POP》时，拉徐一晖来帮忙，那时我正在改写旧稿《毛泽东艺术模式》和《思潮迭起的中国现代艺术》的文字，徐一晖帮我翻拍了大量的图片，他尤其注意到我搜集的近百年中国艺术俗化——从月份牌年画到延安艺术农民化再到文革红光亮的语言线索的图片。此间，他多次和我谈起他对近代俗文化与今天消费文化的关系很感兴趣，那时他还没有人住圆明园艺术村，就已经画了《红宝书》等作品，这是后来的陶瓷《红宝书》、《快餐盒饭》等作品的雏形，时间是1992年的秋天，而且我还把这些作品选作我1992年冬在台湾策划的“政治波普”的展览中，这其实就是最早的艳俗艺术，或者说是艳俗艺术的雏形，因为，徐的《红宝书》依然有政治波普的影响。之后，徐一晖人住圆明园，开始使用满街已经流行了的串灯，创作了《向日葵》、《暖水瓶》等作品，时间是1993年的春天，他这时的作品有的有政治色彩，如向日葵，有的已无政治的痕迹，如暖水瓶。

大卫·拉舍帕尔作品(David. Lachapelle)

与此同时，1993年的冬天，我去重庆看作品，看到四川美术学院研究生俸振杰的《偶像与迷狂》等为题的系列作品，关注的也是消费文化，画面也是艳俗的，联系徐一晖和祁志龙等人的作品，我心里对关注消费文化的作品开始有一点感觉。

此时，真正开始对艳俗艺术开展工作的是徐一晖，他和杨卫、刘峥、王庆松，以及祁志龙等人，在这个阶段里过往从密，应该说，自1993－1994年始，在徐一晖的周围，聚集起一个以关注大众文化为共识的小圈子。1994年，徐一晖跟我谈起他关于陶瓷作品的想法，该年的夏天，我陪徐一晖去了我的家乡磁州窑，见了我的一些做陶瓷的朋友，朋友看了徐一晖的草图后，认为磁州窑的陶瓷材料不适合表现徐的作品，朋友建议我们去景德镇或者佛山试试。后来，我与景德镇的朋友取得联系，该年9月份，徐一晖去了景德镇。1995年初，徐一晖从景德镇烧成作品回来，并回了一趟南京，于是胡向东人住圆明园。是年春天，徐、杨、胡和刘峥、王庆松等人有过多次长谈，很多想法就是在这几次谈话中具体化的，在这个圈子中，杨卫是个思想活跃和喜欢读书、写作的人，他主动担负起写作的工作，他该年年底的《文化崩溃时期的庸俗艺术》的文章，就是在他们的谈话中产生的，当然，其中很多提法也与其他人尤其与徐一晖有关，诸如“民族喜剧风格主义”之类。事实上，徐一晖在景德镇期间，

张培力作品

就在断断续续写作他后来才发表的《现代主义‘精英’与大众文化语境》的文字，

方力均作品

只是他认为艳俗艺术不是什么重要的艺术运动，不存在什么理论问题，重要的是作品。因为除了徐一晖，其他人的作品还没有什么面貌，包括杨卫那时的作品，还是类似李山那种粉红色荷花的东西。他们作品的成型，是在1996年的秋天，我有一次应徐一晖的邀请去了圆明园艺术家村，我看到了他们如胡向东、王庆松等人不约而同画起了艳俗的“萝卜大白菜”，刘峥画了《阳光灿烂的日子》等作品，杨卫画了人民币《中国人民很行》的系列。确切地说，这些作品虽然有了艳俗的倾向，但是这是他们集体讨论的结果，诸如“萝卜大白菜最通俗”，以及把中国人民银行看成“中国人民很行”的流行笑话等等，这只是对大众文化的一种概念化的共识，而不是一种个人的感觉。但这时我开始有了策划一个展览的想法，但当时我觉得他们的作品太雷同，并当面指出了这种雷同的倾向，我当时对他们说，再等等看，待作品有了进展后，再做展览。

但在1996年4月份，王劲松、祁志龙、徐一晖找我和廖雯，想做展览。过了几天，杨卫也来找我和廖雯，也要做展览。我当时想把两拨人合在一起，但没有成功。此前，我已经给俸振杰的展览画册写了《溃烂之处，艳若桃李》的序，在构思徐、王、祁的展览时，开始以“艳俗艺术”的概念称呼他们的作品，并为展览起了《大众样板》的展题。在处理杨卫等人的展览时，杨卫提出展览是否起个与化妆打扮有关的题目，我起了《艳妆生活》的题目。加上俸振杰和后来被封闭的罗氏兄弟的展览，1996年的春天，一连串就有四个展览：4 · 13《艳妆生活》；4 · 20《大众样板》；4 · 27《溃烂之处，艳若桃李》；5 · 18《浮华的伤害》。其实，自1992年我看到徐一晖和祁志龙的作品后，就在考虑如何去把握这种风格的艺术，美国从60年代的波普到80年代的JEFF KOONS，其间的语言转换和区别在什么地方，以及中国从政治波普到艳俗艺术，也经历了同样的过程，那么，中国的艳俗艺术与JEFF KOONS的区别又在什么地方，这是我写艳俗艺术的前两文的用力之处。

宋永红作品

至于艳俗艺术的概念，美国人称JEFF KOONS类的风格为KITSCH，1939年，著名美国艺术批评家格林柏格在一篇著名的文章《前卫或者媚俗（avant-garde or kitsch）》一文中，坚持现代主义艺术的精英立场，把当时兴起的艺术都斥为kitsch。但是，由于60年代美国消费文化和中产阶级的成长，kitsch 成为日常生活用品和大众的基本品味，同时艺术家对这个现实的反讽模仿也成为风气，著名女性主义批评家LUCY.R.LIPPARD写的《粉红色的玻璃天鹅》，恰当地把握了这个现实。尤其安迪 · 沃霍著名的商品变为艺术，艺术变为商品的观点，影响深远，而且安迪 · 沃霍在60年代收藏了很多艳俗的工艺品，在他去世后竟被拍卖了150万美元。90年代以来，更多的批评家开始站在格林柏格的不同的立场上，讨论包括JEFF KOONS、CINDY SHERMAN、BARBARA KRUGER、MIKE KELLEY、JENNY HOLZER、DAVID HAMMONS、ELIZABETH MURRAY在内的当代艺术家的作品。尤其是IRVING SANDLER所著的《后现代时期的艺术（Art of the postmodern era）》尤为著名，书中认为包括JEFF KOONS等人的艺术，颠覆了对现代主义精英艺术眼光的迷信，摆

祁志

脱了现代主义精英对形式主义和崇高品味的迷信，证实在艺术经验里应该有比审美更重要的东西，即在这些艺术家的作品中呈现出了对社会进行批判、建设和破坏性的新倾向。

KITSCH这个词在中国出现，我的印象是，90年代随着米兰·昆德拉的著作翻译被引进的，翻译界译KITSCH为媚俗。米兰·昆德拉对KITSCH 有过详解。KITSCH在我们的英汉词典里只给出“矫揉造作；拙劣的文艺作品”的答案，这是一个源于德语的词，它含庸俗、廉价和老百姓喜欢的那种漂亮东西的意思。1994年，我曾就KITSCH与哈佛大学一位来访问我的博士生作过探讨，当时我们讨论时，我觉得如果作为一种艺术的概念，是否译作“艳俗”更好些，我当时的想法是，艺术是对KITSCH现实的一种反讽，不是KITSCH现实的本身。1996年澳洲的《视觉艺术与文化》刊用了我的《波普之后：艳俗话语与反讽模仿》时，也把艳俗译作KITSCH。我觉得不合适，而且美国90年代初，也没有人使用KITSCH ART作为概念的。1996年在德国的一个会议上，我与美国《现代艺术博物馆》的策展人BARBARA LONDON女士，也曾就此问题作过讨论，而且我请教她，如何就中国的艳俗艺术，找到一个

祁志龙作品

更确切的英文概念，她说她想到中国来看看这些作品，后来她来了中国并看了这些作品后，她觉得英文用GAUDY ART更合适。直到此时，我才从英文和中文上确定了这个概念，但是，我思考这个概念确实经历了几年的时间，因为我觉得概念与把握艺术现象的准确度有关，包括玩世写实主义的概念，我曾在“玩世写实主义”、“泼皮幽默写实主义”、“幽默写实主义”几个概念中犹豫过一段时间。正是从这个角度说，杨卫的“庸俗艺术”不是“艳俗艺术”的前身，使用“艳俗艺术”更不是想找一个概念代替杨卫的“庸俗艺术”，以及徐一晖的“民族喜剧风格主义”等等，这只是各自的不同说法，就象玩世写实主义，王林先生称“异样写实主义”，刘骁纯先生称“强聚焦”，尹吉男先生称“新生代”一样。何况我早在1994年以来，就一直在考虑用“艳俗”代替KITSCH，因为KITSCH就有庸俗的含义，既然90年代美国的批评家不同意格林柏格把JEFF KOONS等人斥为KITSCH，而且，中国的艳俗与JEFF KOONS又有它的不同之处，寻找一个新的概念是自然的。

1999·3·25

徐一晖作品

徐一晖作品

徐一晖作品

Some More Thoughts on the Raison d'Etre of Gaudy Art

★ Li Xianting

In my previous two writings on the subject*, I have pointed out that the concept of Gaudy Art is strongly influenced by American artist Jeff Koons, whose popularity in the art world soared during the 1980's. By the late 1980's and early 1990's essays and exhibition catalogues relating to Koons' work began to enjoy wide-spread circulation in Chinese art circles. Gaudy Art also grew out of the formalistic elements and creative impulses of Chinese Political Pop and Cynical Realism. What I mean by formalistic elements in this respect, is a tendency toward the use of gaudy or garish colors and materials. As early as 1990, the former "Popi" (suggestive of the English word ennui) artist Zhang Peili painted his "Aerobics" series which were unmistakably incorporating such elements in his work. Their use can also be detected in the Political Pop artists, Fang Lijun and Song Yonghong's works as early as 1992. Both Cynical Realism and Political Pop, as forms of "unofficial art", even if they could not be exhibited publicly and thereby gain public acceptance, reflected a "Zeitgeist",its English counterpart being a Spirit of the Age, depiction in the bored ennui, roguish humor, and political irreverence that much of the work displayed.. All of the things which appeared broadly in the literature, music, movies and television serials of the time. There are elements of Political Pop and Cynical Realism which in many ways are interchangeable and overlap. Whether it be Cynical Realism's depiction of "popi", or Political Pop' s use of consumer images and of its toying with political images. The underlying trend was to express a political position, even when the work had no direct relationship with politics. The fact that these works symbolized China in the late 80s and early 90s, encouraged a kind of widespread public sentiment at the time. Cynicism and "popi" have many precedents in Chinese intellectual history, manifesting themselves especially in periods in which there is a high degree of political control. For example, the scholar gentry class in the fourth century, between the Wei and Jin Dynastic reigns, was often portrayed as a self-derisive, crazed rogues who found a way to deal with tight political controls. A well-known literary work of the time, Shi Shuo Xin Yu (literally translated, World Stories New Language), is full of documented examples. Cynical Realism's characteristics on the other hand were a more pedestrian attitude to everyday-life. Plays and essays produced during the thirteenth century Yuan dynasty are filled with examples of "popi" and self-derision. Sun Daya in his seminal work "Tian Lai Ji Xu" used "Cynical Farce" in reference to Bai Pu, a writer of ballads at the time. The sense of ennui and inner-emptiness expressed in this kind of dissolute and " popi" style seems to be a common way for China' s scholar gentry class to find escape in dark political times. Another interesting comparison, is that of one of China's most popular Buddhist images, "Mi Le Buddha," which portrays this important religious icon holding his belly, reeling in good-hearted laughter, which for me is similar in terms of its expressive form and spirit to Fang Lijun's characters. They are often portrayed laughing in a similarly irreverent and almost impious way. However, it was artist Qi Zhilong who, from the beginning, infused his late Political Pop works with popular Gaudy "social flower" motifs, movie stars and poster girl images. Although never overtly political, his works were in many ways the precursors of Gaudy Art. It may even be suggested that he stands as one of the original Gaudy Art artists. From the beginning, he preferred his works to be referred to as "consumer images". This is what I refer to when I say that Gaudy Art's "creative impulses" can be traced to Political Pop art which expressed the deep psychological feelings evoked by the impact of Western consumer culture on socialist political ideology. This becomes more apparent when we look at the images of flashy actresses, beautiful women and social flowers in the works of Qi Zhilong and compare them for example, with Wang Guangyi's "Great Castigation" or Yu Youhan's " Mao and Whitney" both of which are highly representative of Political Pop art. In Qi's works, the political image has been considerably muted while the consumer image is made more prominent. It becomes an important distinction between the "gaudy" tendencies of Political Pop and Cynical Realism and Gaudy Art works themselves. The critical approach of Gaudy Art is not a departure from the past. Rather, Gaudy Art is an attitude that consumer culture and everyday life have taken leave of politics. It is a genuine feeling about the gaudiness and its many appearances that have come with a consumer culture running rampant in China.

Another way to put it might be to say that artists associated with Gaudy Art are intuitively responding to the "get-rich-quick" attitude of the dreams and realities of peasants, brought about or emerging out of the consequences of Western consumer culture in China. Nonetheless, its not consumer culture that is at issue here. Given that modern day consumer culture takes root and grows from the social values and standards of a modernized society, it is a fact that China does not have either the social values and standards or a modernized society that seems central to Gaudy Art. With regard to my position that Gaudy Art is driven by "a peasant-like, get-rich-quick taste, it seems to me that all cultures are founded upon the existence of a set system of social standards and values. Yet, over the past hundred years, as China has broken with its traditional culture and accepted the impact of Western culture, it has still never really approved the value system underlying Western culture. From such early social philosophy as "China as the basic essence, theWest as a means to an end," to "China's basic essence is the socialist ideology", the foundation upon which contemporary culture stands essentially comprises of short-term political pragmatism and expedience. As a result, China has been unable to establish lasting cultural systems and forms. So-called "traditional culture" and even "Western culture" in today's reality are nothing more than attitudes borrowed in the name of such political pragmatism and expedience. Western and traditional cultural forms are mostly employed to serve a political agenda. I don't know if this constitutes culture and so I refer to it as "the culture of convenience". In China's present social structure this attitude allows people in positions of authority to pick and choose from traditional, and Western culture according to their own personal preference, memories or requirements. Culture for these people is forever in an unsystematic state of disparate pieces. For the peasant elements in power, modern consumer culture naturally takes the form of things like "Happiness and Prosperity", "8888" (the number eight sounds like the character "fa" , which means to "get rich") and Red Lanterns. Of course, I'm over-simplifying. Hopefully, the future others will be able to take a closer look at this phenomena.

It is against this backdrop,that China's Gaudy Art being influenced by the art of Jeff Koons can be verified. For me this seems only natural. Each and every artist must work from a certain linguistic tradition or school. The important thing is the artist's feelings and whether they are informed by today's realities, not to mention the manner in which the artist chooses to express his feelings toward this reality. Or, in the case ,of those artist's whose work has been affected by Koons's work, the thing that concerns me most is, how the artist in question turns this into their own mode of discourse?

As already mentioned, Qi Zhilong is an important artist emerging out from Political Pop towards Gaudy Art.. Another important artist is Xu Yihui who was initially involved in the 1985 New Tide Movement, but then subsequently found himself less active for a number of years. Between the years 1991 and 1992, when planning the "Post '89: New Chinese Art "and "Mao Goes Pop" exhibitions, Xu Yihui provided me with additional support. When re-writing "Artistic Renditions of Mao" and "The Layers of New Thought on China's Modern Art". Xu helped me copy and organize countless slides. He began to compare Shanghai Calendar Posters, and Yanan peasant-based art, to later Cultural Revolution's "Red, Bright and Shiny" posters which he felt had led to a form of "debasement" of Chinese culture. At that time, Xu spoke to me on a number of occasions about the relationship between consumer culture and this steady debasement or "vulgarization" of culture over the past hundred years. At the time, he had not yet moved to the artist colony at Yuan Ming Yuan outside Beijing. He had, however, already completed his painting, "The Little Red Book", a precursor of his porcelain works such including,"Fast Food Lunch Box". It was in the fall of 1992 that I decided to include these works in a Political Pop exhibition I was curating in Taiwan at the time. In fact, I felt these works to be the earliest works of Gaudy Art. Or to put it another way, these works were the precursor forms of Gaudy Art because works like "Little Red Book" had been very much influenced by Political Pop art. After moving to Yuan Ming Yuan in the Spring of 1993, Xu began work on "Sunflower", "Warm Water Bottle" and other works. He employed such objects as strings of "twinkle" lights popular outside the entrances of stores and restaurants at the time. Some of Xu's early works, unlike "Warm Water Bottle" "Sunflower," still had political overtones .

At the end of 1993, I had the chance to go to the Chongqing region where I saw works by a recent graduate of the Sichuan Art Academy, Feng Zhengjie, His work such as his "Idols and Zealotry", also focused on consumer culture. The canvases were bright and gaudy in color. They recalled the works of Xu Yihui and Qi Zhilong. It was then for the first time, that I began to gain a feeling for works concerned with consumerism and the debasement of culture.

At the time, Xu Yihui had embarked wholeheartedly on the production of Gaudy Art works. Along with Yang Wei, Liu Zheng and Qi Zhilong, Xu and others who met frequently. I should say that in the period from 1993 to 1994, a group of artists with common interests emerged around Xu Yihui and his works. In 1994, Xu Yihui told me about his idea for a series of porcelain works. That summer, I accompanied him to the Ci Zhou Porcelain Kiln in my home town where I introduced him to some porcelain artisans who were friends of mine. After seeing his sketches and understanding his requirements, they suggested that he might be better served by the Porcelain kilns in Jingdezhen. During September, on my introduction, he went to Jingdezhen for the first time. By early 1995, he had completed his first porcelain works and returned to Nanjing. About the same time, Hu Xiangdong moved into the artist colony at Yuan Ming Yuan. By the Spring of that same year, Xu Yihui, Yang Wei, Hu Xiangdong, Liu Zheng and Wang Qingsong began interacting again. The long talks they had on the subject helped to crystallize their feelings regarding their work. Among the many members of the group, Yang Wei was the writer. He was thoughtful and read lot of books. He took it upon himself to record some of the things happening at the time through his essays and notes. Toward the end of 1995, he finished writing "Vulgar

Arts in a Collapsing Culture". This essay came out of the many talks he had with other artists. Of course, many of these concepts were shared by the other artists, especially Xu Yihui with such works as the "Stylization of Local Theater" In fact, Xu Yihui was hard at work at the time on an article he later published entitled "The Quality of Modernism Versus the Linguistic Realms of Popular Culture" In this article, Xu made the point that he didn't think Gaudy Art was an important artistic movement in the traditional sense. There was no underlying theoretical basis for it. The important thing for him was the resonance of the work itself. Still, with the exception of Xu Yihui's works, other artists had not really taken on a "face". Even Yang Wei's works at the time were similar to the pink lotus works of Political Pop artist Li Shan. Gaudy Art really did not take a definable shape until the Fall of 1996. At the invitation of Xu Yihui, I visited the artists' colony again and saw for the first time the brash gaudy motifs of "turnip and cabbage" of the artists Hu Xiangdong and Wang Qingsong. Liu Zheng had just completed his "Blue Sky Days" work and Yang Wei was working on a series of Renminbi currency works entitled "The Chinese People's Bank". While these works were outwardly gaudy resulting in titles such as "Cabbage and Turnips are Today's Vulgarity" and the "Chinese People's' Bank" along with other such crude jokes, much of the work was still only a reflection of the group's common understanding and conceptualization of mass culture, rather than dealing with personal feelings. Still, I wanted to try to organize an exhibition on the theme. This was despite the feeling that these works were still dangerously similar in both look and feel. After talking to them further and expressing my reservations, I decided to shelve the idea for awhile.

In April of 1996, Wang Xingsong, Qi Zhilong and Xu Yihui sought out both Liao Wen and myself to help them organize an exhibition. A few days later, Yang approached us separately to plan an exhibition for him. At the time I considered putting them all together in one exhibition, but at the time I felt the idea would not work. I had previously written a catalogue essay for Feng Zhengjie entitled "Brightly Colored Plum and Peach Blossoms Among the Ruins". As I thought more about an exhibition for Xu Yihui, Wang Qingsong and Qi Zhilong, I began to refer to their works as "gaudy" in as much as they were garishly colored and using vulgarization as themes in their work. I eventually settled on an exhibition which I titled "Model for the Masses". When planning Yang Wei' s exhibition, I was asked if I could come up with a title that had something to do with dressing up or cosmetics and, for that I chose to use "Rouge Life". If you add to these two exhibitions the solo exhibition of the works of Feng Zhengjie, including an exhibition that was eventually closed down of the Luo Brothers, the Spring of 1996 saw four exhibitions of Gaudy Art: "Rouge Life" on April 13; "Model for the Masses" on April 20; "Brightly Colored Peach and Plum Blossoms Among the Ruins" on April 27; and, "The Damage From the Flooding of China": (a play on the word "fuhua" which means "enriching of China") on May 18.

Since seeing Qi Zhilong and Xu Yihui work I have been trying to get my head around this style of art of art from China. As the US moved from Pop Art in the sixties to Jeff Koons and kitsch in the eighties, how had the visual and verbal language of art changed between the time these two different styles emerged? Were there parallels in the transition from Political Pop to Gaudy Art in Chinese contemporary art? What made Gaudy Art different from the art of Jeff Koons? These were just some of the questions I attempted to address in my previous two articles on the subject.*

I'd like to sum up with a few words on the origin of the term "Gaudy Art" and its meaning. The term "kitsch" and its appropriation into American art can be traced back to 1939 (maybe even further, I'm not sure) when Clement Greenberg wrote his influential essay, "Avant-Garde and Kitsch". Greenberg maintained, what later became a modernist tenet, that art had to have an essential "quality" to be considered art. Anything lacking this "quality" was kitsch. In the nineties, a good number of critics take exception to Greenberg's concept of "quality". This is perhaps most evident in later discussions of the works of Jeff Koons, Cindy Sherman, Barbara Kruger, Mike Kelly, Jenny Holzer, David Hammons, Elizabeth Murray. Critics like Robert Storr point out that artists like Koons effectively debunked the "cult of quality" and " the mystique of the eye"(Art in the Postmodern Era, Irving Sandler, Harper Collins(1996), P. 7). In distancing themselves from modernism's blind faith in formalism, such artists were essentially saying that there ought to be something more important than the aesthetic form of art itself. Thus, we see in works by Koons and similar artists the emergence of social criticisms, some positive, some negative, but all engaged with their surroundings.

The term "kitsch" appeared in China for the first time, if my impression is correct, in the 1990's with the translations of works by Czech writer Milan Kundera. Here the word was translated "meisu" ("mei" meaning "seductively beautiful" and "su" meaning "common, base or vulgar"). In the English - Chinese dictionaries, kitsch is defined "clumsy or crude handicrafts; cheaply made." The term originated from Germany, where I understand it implied something common or cheap, or even something pretty that was popular with the people. I had a chance to sit down and discuss the subject of kitsch with a Harvard scholar in 1994. We agreed that a more accurate translation might be "yansu" ("yan" meaning "garrishly or brightly colored" and "su" meaning "common, base or vulgar"). However, my thinking at the time was that the art I was experiencing was really a parody of kitsch. It was not kitsch itself. This term "yansu" had come up with was translated into the word "kitsch", for a speech I gave at "Visual Art and Culture" in Australia in 1996. Entitled "Popu Zhihou: Yansu Yuyan yu Fanfeng Mofang" - it was translated as "After Political Pop: Kitsch Discourse and Satirical Parody". Looking back, I don't think this translation of "yansu" was accurate. During that same year I also had an opportunity to talk with New York MOMA curator, Barbara London, on the subject. I asked her if she could think of a term that might be more accurate in meaning. After seeing the works first hand, we agreed that her term "Gaudy Art" might be more appropriate. As American critics today disagree with Greenberg position that art produced like that of Koons should be considered kitsch, similarly I don't think the "yansu" art produced by those artists whose work have been discussing should be considered kitsch. It seemed only natural to search for a new term to describe this kind of art emerging in China.

1999.3.25

* The title of Li's previous two articles on the subject of Gaudy Art are : After Political Pop: Kitsch Discourse and Satirical Parody" and "Parodying 'Peasant StyleFrom - Wed .

艺术史
陶瓷
Art History,1999
Porcelain
200 × 100 × 50cm

金钱
陶瓷 金水
Golden Money, 1998-1999
Porcelain
38 × 30 × 22cm

☞ 理想种植
树脂
Dream Plants ,1999
Resin

水晶白菜
树脂
Crystal Cabbage, 1999
Resin
45 × 40 × 36cm

理想家居(一)
布面油彩
Dream Household Belongings No.1,1999
Oil on Canvas
162 × 130cm

理想家居(二)
布面油彩
Dream Household Belongings No.2,1999
Oil on Canvas
162 × 130cm

浪漫旅程

布面油彩

Romantic Journey Series NO. 21,1997

Oil on Canvas

150 × 190cm

浪漫旅程

布面油彩

Romantic Journey Series NO. 22,1998

Oil on Canvas

110 × 110cm

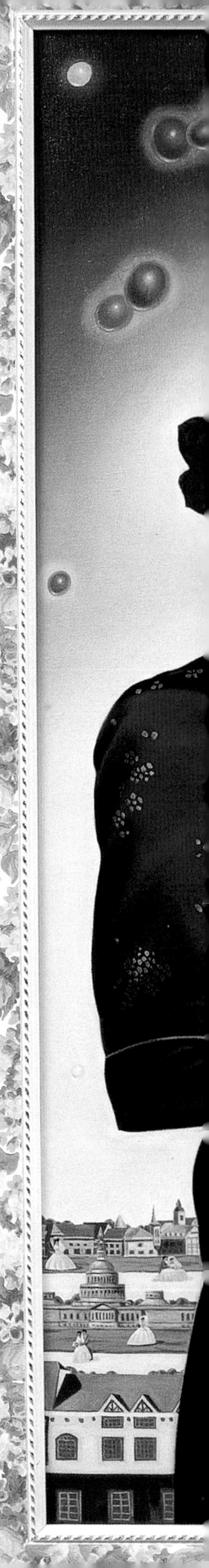

☝浪漫旅程

布面油彩

Romantic Journey Series NO. 26,1999

Oil on Canvas

150 × 190cm

☞浪漫旅程

布面油彩

Romantic Journey Series NO. 23,1998

Oil on Canvas

110 × 110cm

FENGZHENJIE No.23

千手拿来观音☞

仿丝绸布面 工业油彩

Thousand Hands Buddha,1999

Spray Paint on Velvet

200 × 120cm

思想者☜

仿丝绸布面 工业油彩

The Thinker,1998

Spray Paint on Velvet

200 × 100cm

王 庆松
WANG QINGSONG

Marlboro
燕京啤酒
Yanjing Beer

亚当与夏娃
仿丝绸布面 工业油彩
Adam & Eve,1998
Spray Paint on Velvet
188 × 120cm

老兵与新兵
仿丝绸布面 工业油彩
Old Soldiers & New Soldiers,1997
Spray Paint on Velvet
176 × 120cm

罗氏兄弟
LUO BROTHERS

欢迎世界名牌
漆画
Welcome World Famous Brands Series,1999
Lacquer Painting
126 × 246cm

可口可乐
Coca-Cola

欢迎世界名牌

漆画

Welcome World Famous Brands Series,1999

Lacquer Painting

66 × 55cm × 12

欢迎世界名牌

漆画

Welcome World Famous Brands Series,1999

Lacquer Painting

66 × 55cm

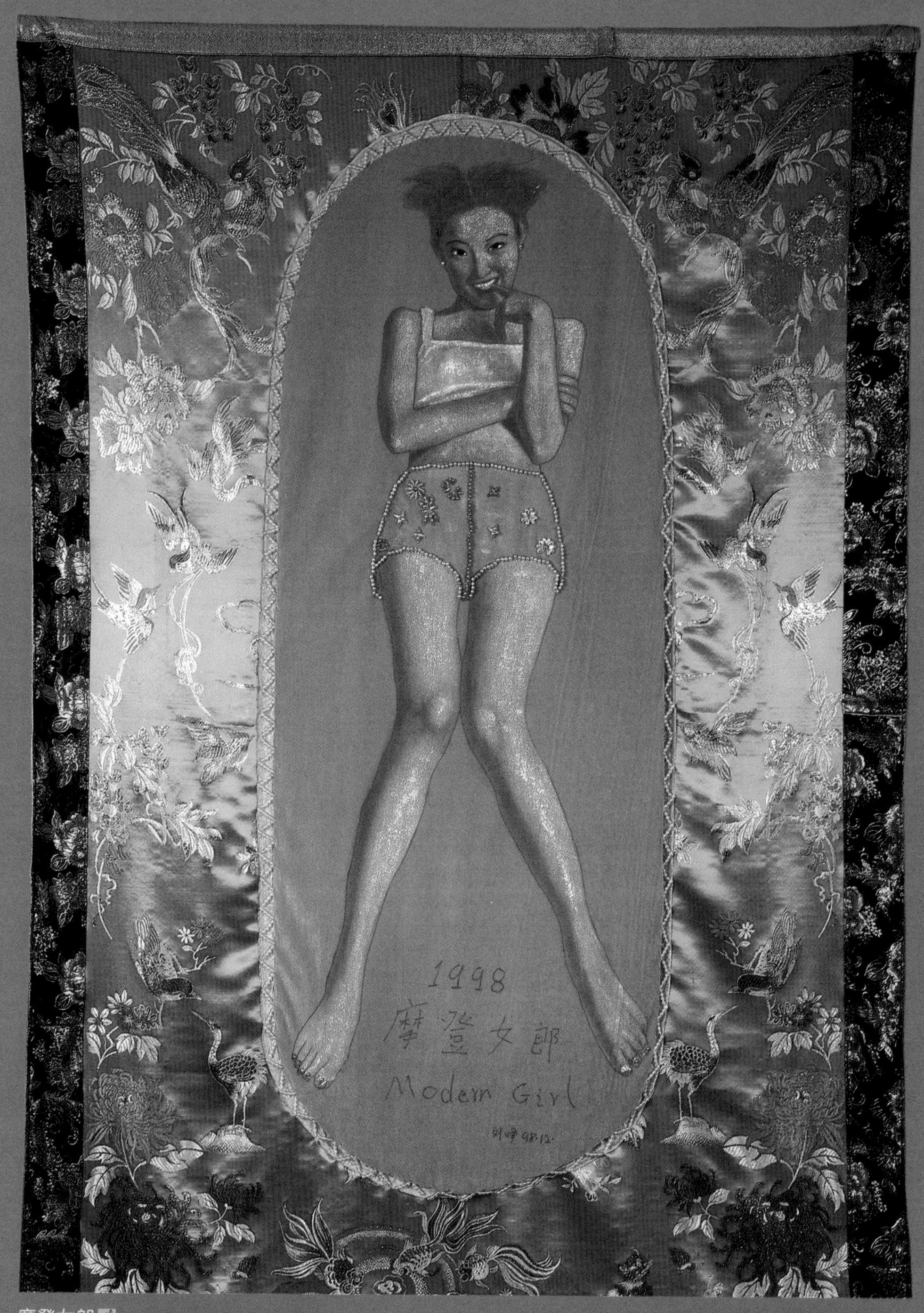

摩登女郎

珠子 被面 绒布 丙烯

Modern Womany,1999

Beads and Acrylic on Brocade

180 × 140cm

仿月份牌

珠子 被面 绒布 丙烯

Imitation Calendar, 1998

Beads and Acrylic on Brocade

180 × 130cm

刘 峥
LIU ZHENG

刘 峥
LIU ZHENG

☝ 庐山恋

珠子 被面 绒布 丙烯

Love in the Lu Mountains,1998

Beads and Acrylic on Brocade

200 × 140cm

☜ 月

珠子 被面 绒布 丙烯

The Moon, 1998

Beads and Acrylic on Brocade

210 × 150cm

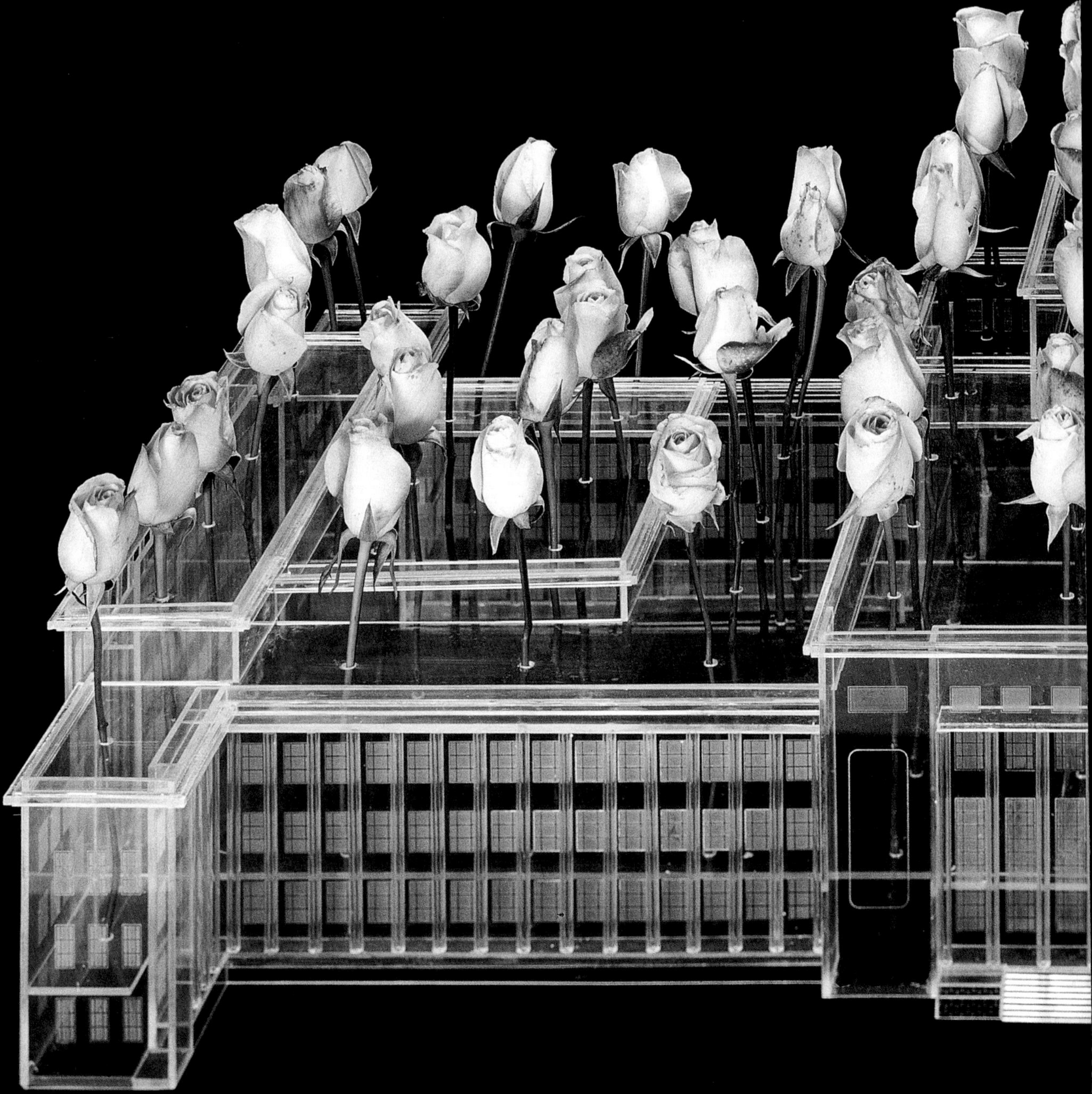

有机玻璃 花

Flower, 1998

Plexi Glass and Fresh Flowers

112 × 75 × 25cm

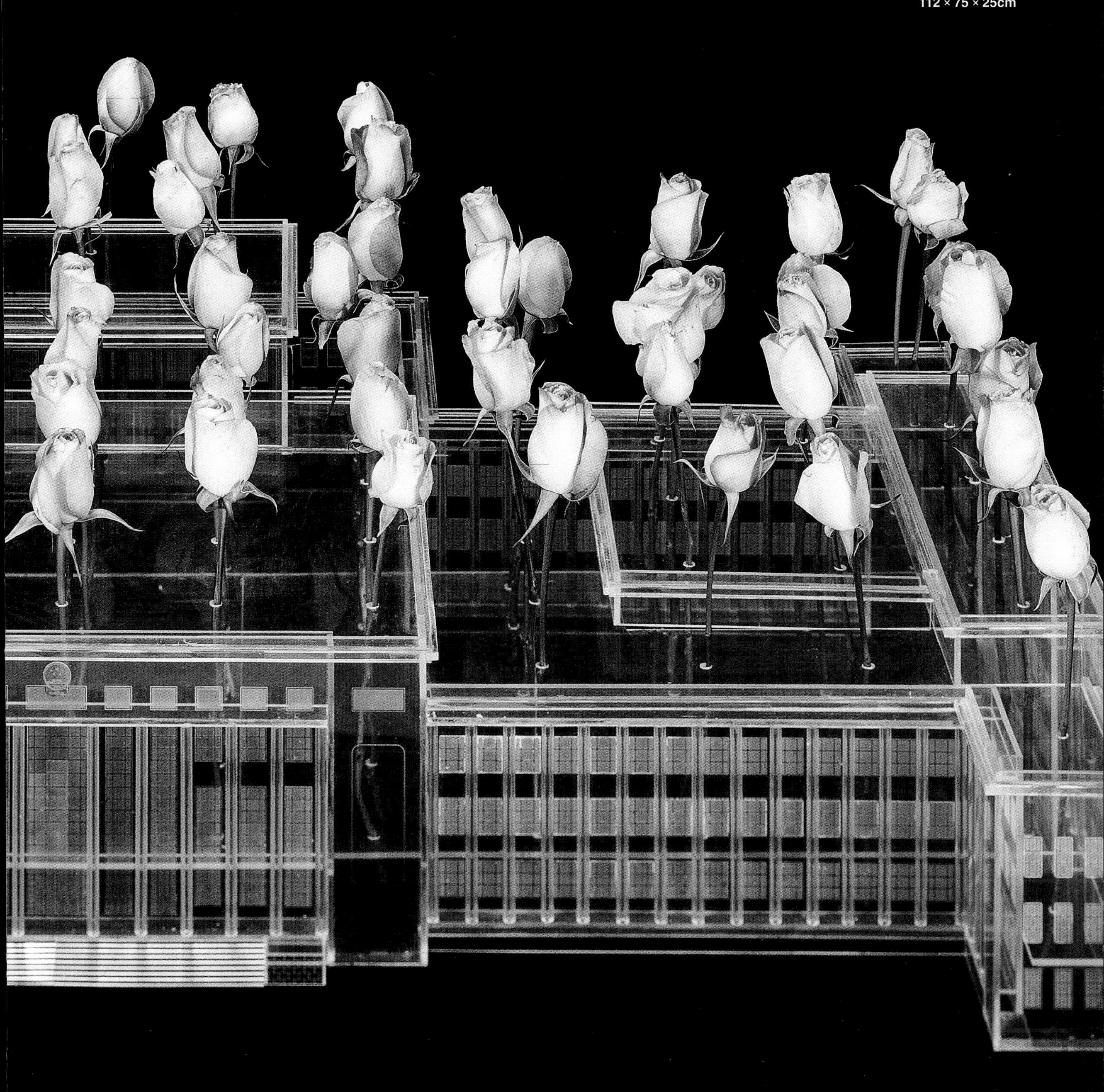

花鸟鱼虫系列之二　鸟笼
有机玻璃 鸟
Bird, 1998
Plexi Glass and Live Birds
90 × 45 × 55cm

花鸟鱼虫系列之四　虫罐
有机玻璃 蝈蝈
Bugs, 1999
Poleax Glass and Live Grasshoppers
58 × 33 × 30cm

花鸟鱼虫系列之一　鱼缸
有机玻璃 鱼
Fish, 1998
Poleax Glass and Goldfish
90 × 55 × 28.5cm

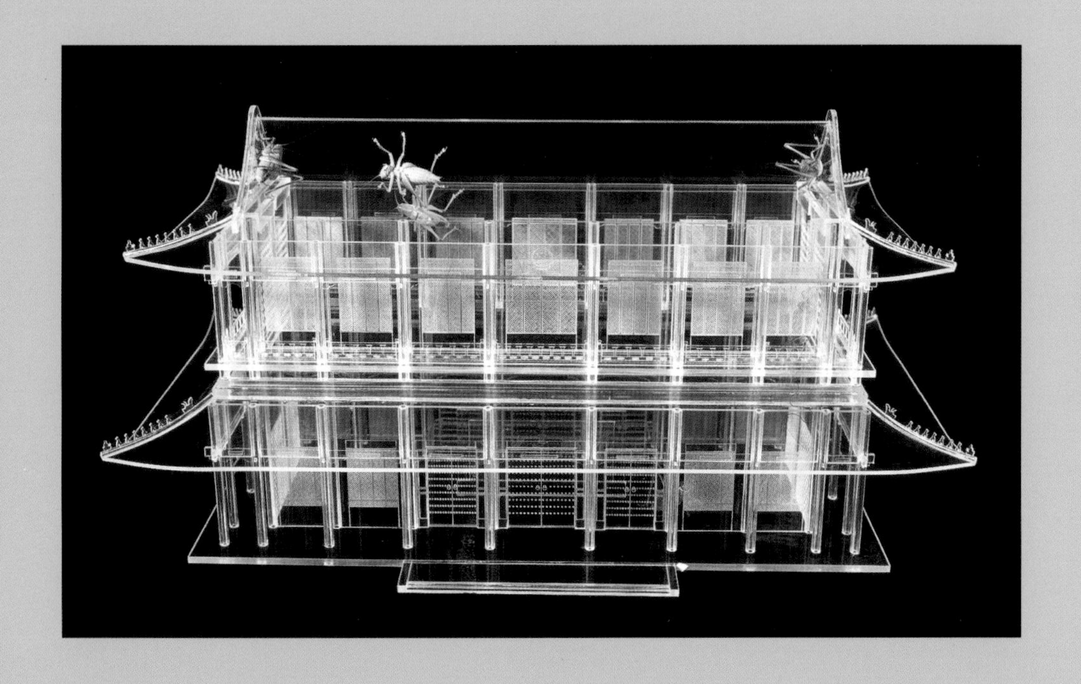

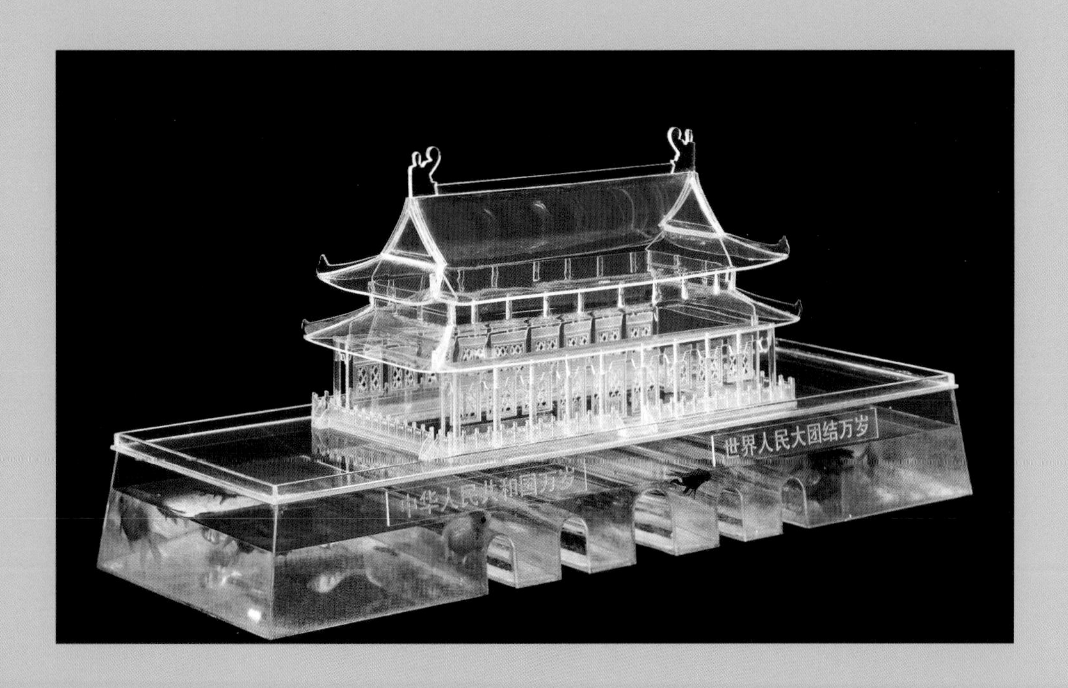
世界人民大团结万岁
中华人民共和国万岁

典型
丙烯 玻璃钢 油漆
Model Standards Series, 1998
Glass Fiber, Oil and Acrylic
55 × 42cm × 9

典型 NO.7
丙烯 玻璃钢 油漆
Model Standards Series, 1998
Glass Fiber, Oil and Acrylic
55 × 42cm

邵 振鹏
SHAO ZHENPENG

中国制造
仿红木
Made in China Series, 1999
Imitation Rosewood
57.5 × 46 × 96cm × 2
74 × 60.5 × 116cm

中国制造
仿红木
Made in China Series, 1999
Imitation Rosewood
57.5 × 46 × 96cm

中国制造
仿红木
Made in China Series, 1999
Imitation Rosewood
74 × 60.5 × 116cm

邵振鹏
SHAO ZHENPENG

便宜
摄影
Cheep, 1999
Photograhy
120 × 120cm

便宜
摄影
Cheep, 1999
Photograhy
120 × 120cm

便宜
摄影
Cheep, 1999
Photograhy
120 × 120cm

便宜
摄影
Cheep, 1999
Photograhy
120 × 120cm

小姐系列—前卫艺术小姐
玻璃钢 陶瓷 即时贴 生活用品
Miss Series, Miss Advant Guarde,1998
Manaquin with objects

孙平
SUN PING

Hali-Hali Happy

孙平
SUN PING

小姐系列—为你服务小姐

玻璃钢 陶瓷 即时贴 生活用品

Miss Series, Miss Service,1998

Manaquin with objects and Porcelain

小姐系列—文化时尚小姐

玻璃钢 陶瓷 即时贴 生活用品

Miss Series, Miss Fashion Culture,1999

Manaquin with objects

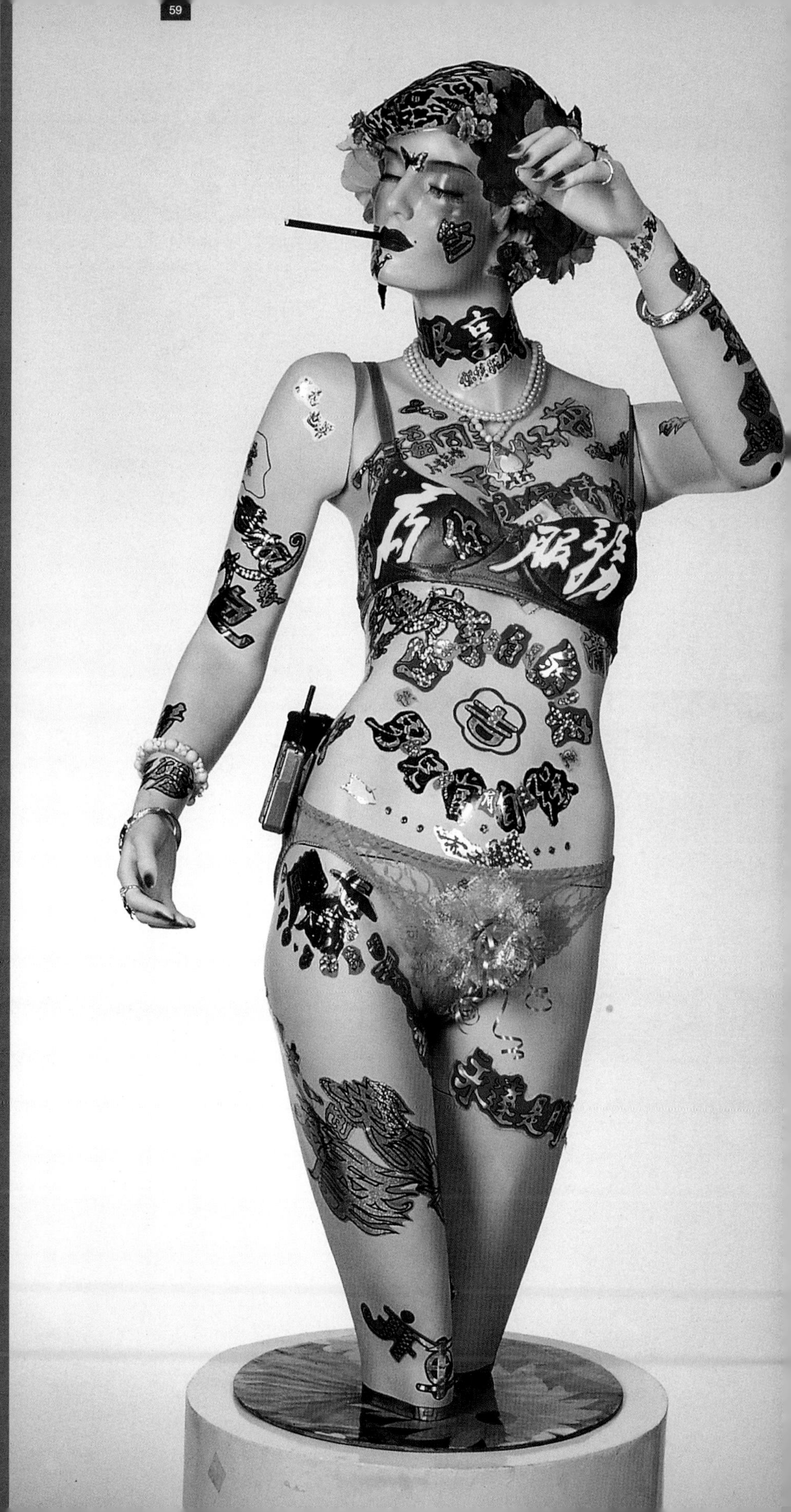

中国手姿
布面油彩
Chinese Jewery Series No.3,1996
Oil on Canvas
146 × 144cm

中国手姿
布面油彩
Chinese Jewery Series No.13,1998
Oil on Canvas
200 × 180cm

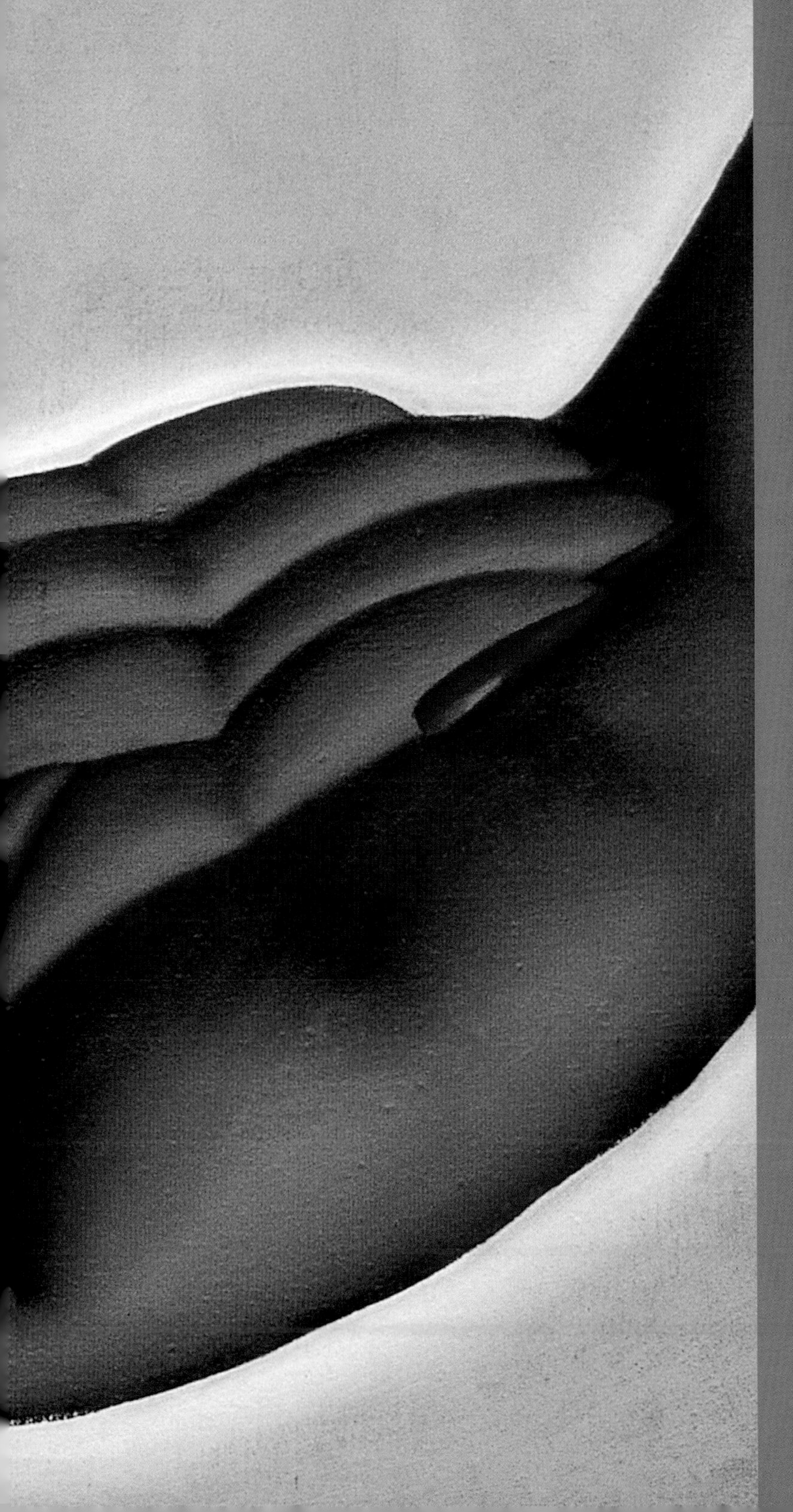

中国手姿
布面油彩
Chinese Jewery Series No.15,1998
Oil on Canvas
114 × 146cm

中国手姿
布面油彩
Chinese Jewery Series No.10,1997
Oil on Canvas
120 × 122cm

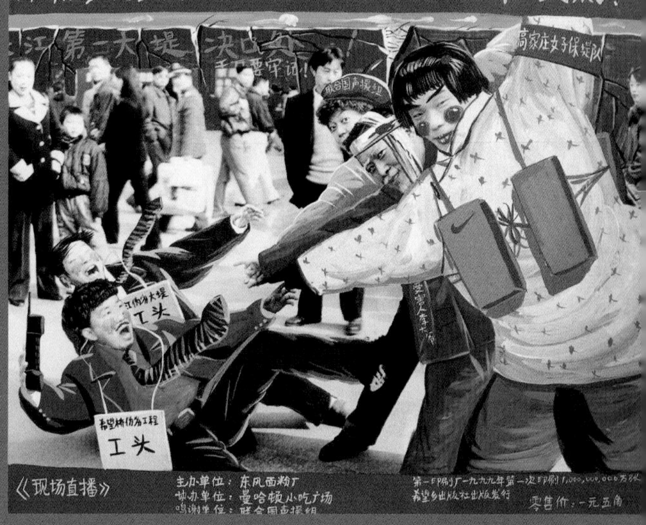

现场直播

照片 丙烯

Live Broadcast,1999

Acrylic on Photography

50 × 40cm × 4

赵勤 刘健
ZHAO QIN LIU JIAN

赵勤 刘健
ZHAO QIN LIU JIAN

我爱麦当劳
照片 丙烯
I Love McDonalds,1998
Acrylic on Photography
50 × 40cm × 4

长满毛发的大便
丝绸
Shit with Hair,1999
Brocade and Cotton
40 × 40 × 40cm

满怀理想的大便
丝绸
Shit with a Dream1999
Brocade and Cotton
40 × 40 × 60cm

经典
陶瓷
Porcelain
Live Broadcast,1999
32 × 29 × 26cm

经典
陶瓷
Porcelain
Live Broadcast,1999
59 × 39cm

刘 力国
LIU LIGUO

捍卫地球的洛克人
油彩 电脑输出
Luke, The Earth Protector,1998
Computer Printout in Oil Painting
217 × 335cm

吉普赛姑娘
油彩 电脑输出
Gypsy Girl,1999
Computer Printout in Oil Painting
204 × 326cm

捍卫地球的洛克人
油彩 电脑输出
Luke, The Earth Protector,1998
Computer Printout in Oil Painting
217 × 335cm

吉普赛姑娘
油彩 电脑输出
Gypsy Girl,1999
Computer Printout in Oil Painting
204 × 326cm

杨 茂林
YANG MAOLIN

天作之合

塑钢(ABS) 电脑输出 画布

Born to be Together - Gun,1998

Painting with Object

枪H140cm

画194 × 112cm

198了解红萝卜的N种方法

LED BOAPD+FRP

装置

The N Method of Understanding A Carrot,1998

Installation

恶恶霸与天堂刀

即兴表演

Villain and Hypocrite,1997

Performance

挥长鞭

Raised Staff for Bcating

1997

做人做事要正當
背痛貼正光
製藥有限公司
2001年1月1日
西海岸海產
百利

顾 世勇
GU SHIYONG

2001年1月1日　回家的路上
电脑动画装置
January 1st, 2001—On the Road Home,1998
Installation
2001年1月1日　回家的路上
即兴表演
January 1st, 2001—On the Road Home,1999
Performance

龙来了
摄影
The Dragon is Coming,1998
Photography
120 × 180cm

春丽
摄影
Chunli,1998
Photography
120 × 180cm

春丽（站立）
Chunli (Standing),1998
Photography
120 × 180cm

美少女战士
Pretty Girl Soldier ,1998
Photography
120 × 180cm

对"农民式的暴发趣味"的仿讽

——中国艳俗艺术语境述评续补

★ 栗宪庭

自1996年年上半年《艳妆生活》、《大众样板》展之后，从事艳俗艺术的艺术家们仍继续着自己的工作，上次展览所暴露出语言雷同和不到位，促使这些艺术家们都力图完善或开拓自己的话语方式。而且我们不断看到一些艳俗倾向或关注消费文化的新艺术家的出现。诸如湖南的李路明、孙平，四川的余极，福建的袁文彬，以及广州《卡通一代》的艺术家群等。

关注艳俗和消费文化的艺术家的不断出现，说明艳俗艺术依然是当代文化问题中的一个针对点。艳俗艺术在语言上受过JEEF KOONS的影响，但是这种影响是一种启发，启发了中国艺术家不能忽视中国当代艳俗文化极度泛滥的现实。我们主张当代艺术家的知识分子角色，但他不应是象牙塔里的精英。艺术无法改变社会，而批判的姿态也不止一种。艳俗艺术的仿讽，不是投合大众艳俗趣味，它只是证明了艺术对现实的无力，当鄙视、批判并不能改变大众艳俗趣味时，现实却显示出它对艺术的强烈影响，艺术家几乎只能证明我们生活在充溢艳俗趣味的时代中这个事实，并在模仿、提示时代的这个侧面时，保持了一点反讽的独立立场，除此之外，我们能奢望艺术对艳俗文化作哪些更有力的批判呢？这使我想起当年的陈独秀，他疾呼打倒文人雅画，力倡通俗写实，但当上海月份牌年画，以极其媚俗的写实方式，描写新女性、新生活方式时，陈独秀却投以鄙视的目光，有点叶公好龙的味道。问题是，清末自郎世宁引写实主义入中国工笔画，中国的艺术乃至生活方式，在丢弃了文人雅文化之后，俗文化在百年之内象潮水一样浸透了我们生活的每一个角落，而且这正是五四新文化的结果。（参看拙作《五四"美术革命"批判》，《毛泽东艺术模式概说》）

徐一晖作品

在现代国家形成之前，贵族文化一直是国家的主宰，诸如中国士大夫文化——琴、棋、书、画、茶、园林之类，不但成为社会正统的审美趣味，而且在相当程度上影响了俗文化，而俗文化只是在一定范围内通行,如中国民间木版年画，只是在农村通行。俗文化主宰社会的审美风气，是现代社会的成果。事实上，中国的俗文化是通过自上而下的途径，代替士文化的，自清末康、梁始，到五四时期的陈独秀、瞿秋白、鲁迅等人，都是从国家救亡图强的角度，把矛头对准文人传统的。因为他们要求唤起民众，所以针对文人传统的高雅，他们力倡艺术的通俗化。作为共产党的领导人，瞿秋白并且身体力行，到苏区开展通俗化的艺术活动。略晚于月份牌年画的是延安文艺运动，1943年，毛泽东发表了《在延安文艺座谈会上的讲话》，为延安文艺运动指明了方向——向农民和农民的艺术学习，才能创造为工农兵喜闻乐见的新风格。轰轰烈烈的延安文艺运动所创造的艺术作品，诸如音乐《黄河大合唱》，歌剧如《白毛女》，美术如古元的木刻等，无一不是汲取了农民艺术的风格。

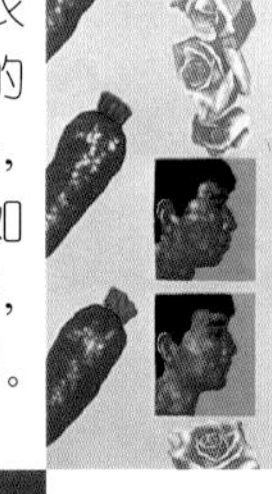

胡

徐一晖作品

这当然并非原本的农民的艺术，尽管如此，作为一种审美趣味，农民的艺术，开始成为由国家主张的可借鉴的主要源泉和样板，取代了文人雅士的趣味。

随着商业广告产生的月份牌年画，其源头虽然与西方写实主义有关，但写实主义直到清末仍为文人所不取，认为"非雅赏"（张浦心）。这是

祁志龙作品

胡向东作品

朗士宁不得不汲取中国画线条、平光的造型方法创作的原因，朗取中揉西的风格又影响了清末的工艺油画，这种工艺油画，又淡化了为文人与专家所欣赏的笔触表现性——这点正是文人画与西方油画都强调的东西，因此写实油画便被转换成一种中国式的通俗风格。月份牌年画使用炭精粉和水彩的方法，更加发展和完善了一种光滑、鲜艳、漂亮和喜庆的风

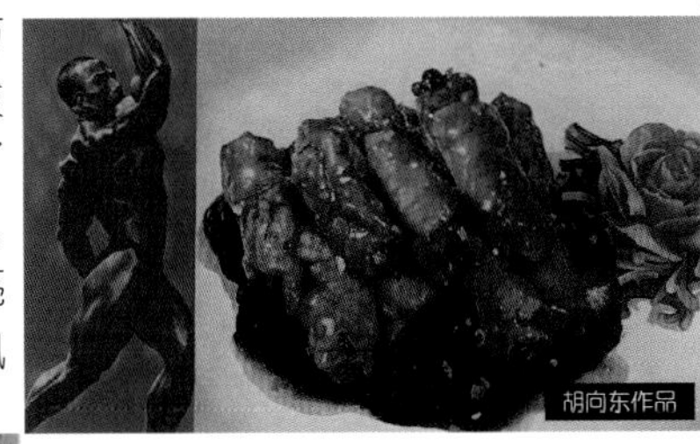
胡向东作品

胡向东作品

格，而且由于它配合了中国的新年和大批量印刷，使其成为更加通俗的画种，以至于1949年后，月份牌年画迅速普及到广大农村，取代了木版年画的地位。1958年，一些美术工作者曾对月份牌年画垄断市场的现象作了调查，结论认为“群众喜欢鼓鼻子鼓眼的造型，喜欢风格很光、很干净。”（薄松年）“年画不但是为了美化，还要图个吉利。”（毛再生，引文集见1958年《美术》四月号、六月号）。

50年代初，国家曾组织过大规模的年画运动，许多著名的油画家、版画家都参与了这个运动，当时的年画风格是勾线加立体造型，介于木板年画与月份牌年画之间。几乎同时，董希文创作出了有年画风格的《开国大典》。其后的若干年，我们接受了苏联的影响，除了反映新生活、为党的路线服务外，重要是加强了写实的基本功，另外戏剧化的情节性，给中国艺术带来很大影响，其实，情节性正是宋元以后的中国文人画抛弃的东西，但它一直保留在民间艺术中，诸如木板年画中的“戏出”等。因为情节性就是“生活本来样式”，因为它本来就具通俗性。尽管如此，1957年的反右活动，还是给了学苏一边倒予很大的冲击，1958年，国家又大张旗鼓地重提延安传统，重提

胡向东作品

民族风格。包括前面提到的给艺术界一向瞧不起的月份牌年画正名等等。1958年，中央美术学院附中全体教师再次创作了具有年画风格的油画《当代英雄》。直到文革艺术的红光亮，这条线索十分清晰。至此，由迎合大众的消费途径发展而来的月份牌年画，与国家意识形态化的吸收农民艺术而来的国家正统艺术，在趣味和审美价值观上合流。

合流的原因有三：一，毛泽东接受列宁关于文艺是党的革命机器上的螺丝钉的观点，而革命的重要策略是发动群众，因此为教育团结人民，自然要求文艺为工农兵喜闻乐见，而工人以及军队的成分，大多来自农民，因此为工农兵也即为农民。二，毛泽东及其共产党的领导阶层，也大多来自农民，自然上下一致。三，列宁曾经说过，革命的胜利就是人民的节日。共产党夺取政权之后，象庆祝节日一样欢庆胜利，而中国的最大节日就是过年，农村过年最红火，因此，红光亮以及与年画有关的喜庆风格，就是在与世界完全隔离的状态下，不断地陶醉在自己制造的种种“人类伟大胜利”的欢乐中诞生的。

这种艺术与审美观的转换，是通过以无产阶级政治专政为核心的阶级斗争的意识形态实现的。辛亥革命和五四运动，从物质和思想上给了士大夫文化以重创。共产党取得胜利后，田地财产的重新分配，士大夫文化的主体——残存的贵族、乡绅、旧式文人，连同近代新兴的资产阶级、暴发户，一起被打倒，士大夫文化及其生活方式的社会物质基础也就被彻底摧毁了。1949年后的一次又一次的政治运动，破四旧，立四新，士大夫文化的思想基础也被清除殆尽。而且，1949年后，铲除的不仅是士大夫文化，还包括五四运动以来的资产阶级新思想。破旧立新，灭资兴无，往后

打士大夫文化，往前打资产阶级文化，所剩的就只是无产阶级文化了。而无产阶级文化的实质，即如前面提到的合流——以国家意识形态为核心，并由国家意识形态转换出的农民文化形态。除此之外，就社会主流文化而言，我们没有创造任何有价值体系的文化形态。因此，1949年以来，运动不断，潮流迭起，而每一种潮流的震源都来自政治变化，每一种潮流又波及生活的方方面面。仅举城市建设为例，50年代大规模拆除旧城墙、旧建筑，为的是“打碎一个旧世界，建设一个新世界。”具体看天安门广场的改造，拆除了大清门和千步廊，就原来设计思想的角度看，紫禁城已不完整，而广场扩大了，那是为了国家检阅军队和群众游行——来自苏联模式——的意识形态的需要。70年代每一个城市都模仿人民大会堂和天安门广场建立了纪念堂和广场，同时每一个城镇的角落都矗立着标语牌和毛主席的雕像。80年代开放以来，一会儿某领导要现代化，高楼便拔地而起，一会儿某领导说要民族化，楼顶便戴上小帽子。今天北京扩展长安街，明天就会在每一个城市一个类似长安街的街道。今天北京盖了几座镜面玻璃高楼，明天就会在全国每一个城市看到玻璃高楼。今天流行瓷砖，明天瓷砖就会贴满全中国大大小小的房子。在中国几乎所有的大城市，你都看不到完整的城市建筑的历史和文化的脉络，看到的只是意识形态的痕迹，以及完全没有任何文化价值支撑的庸俗不堪的房子和街景。在当今城市建设中，残存的传统民居依然不断地遭到破坏自不必说，新建筑的“穿靴戴帽”，也不过是简单庸俗地搬用了传统的某些符号。至于现代建筑，既无细节可看，更无可看的整体造型，我们没有现代化建筑所依赖的现代艺术对造型构成的研究、对材料美感的研究等文化的基础，因为我们从来就是反对现代艺术及其审美价值的。我们要民族风格，却丢掉了自己的传统，我们要现代化，却拒绝现代审美观念。

国家意识形态及其主体——来自农民的无产阶级的领导层，为革命的胜利自然找到了表达它的表现形式——火红与通俗，1949年到70年代末，我们被火红的色彩和简单易懂的口号所包围，哪怕日常使用的茶杯、书包、床单，都会用红旗和口号来装饰。80年代开放以来，几十年来建立的革命价值观，在大众心中失落。随之港台轻松的流行文化乘虚而入，歌星、影星代替了革命英雄而成为青少年心中的偶像。其实，在伴随着西方精英文化涌入中国的同时，西方消费文化也随着合资企业及其产品——影视、时装、流行歌曲、快餐等——从日用品、食品到视觉、听觉，几乎全面渗透到了中国大众的衣食住行的各个方面。精英文化还没来得及喘息，经济大潮便在90年代上半期达到空前的高涨。但是，在这浮华的背后，只是五光十色的发财梦想，而且是通过西方消费文化转换为中国农民式的发财梦想的。于是，把压制太久的财神爷给请出来之后，福禄寿禧，荣华富贵，财源茂盛，8888，乘着经济大潮的东风借尸还魂，红色——这个标志中国农民的喜庆的色彩，在完成了其革命的历史使命之后，又重新粉墨登场：大红灯笼代替了红旗，各种红色广告和标牌代替了红色标语。霓虹灯这个西方消费文化创造出来的兴奋剂，在中国几乎是清一色的以红为主的大红大绿，花里胡哨。这种趣味同时反映在我们的日用品、家具、服装、建筑上，无论我们走到那里，看到什麽，几乎都会碰到花里胡哨的东西，甚至

连电器这种引进的洋玩意儿，都会在上面装饰上五彩的闪光装置，常常让人哭笑不得。

这种红火与花哨即是一种农民式的暴发趣味，所谓暴发，一方面，即这种红火作为喜庆的象征语言，脱离了农民文化原有的质朴的语境。象一夜之间“发了财”，质朴变成没有根底的浮化。其二，暴发的趣味把红火作为表征，是一种没有审美价值转换的现实功利性的直接流露，它先是通过国家意识形态，继而通过消费文化这种现实力量召唤出来的，不属于传统或现代的任何一种审美价值体系，所以它呈现出的是一种即时性、功利性和浮华特征。其中现代设计作为现代社会审美文化的价值支点之一，是经历了由精英文化参与的整个社会审美观的价值转换。诸如霓红灯日用品等审美趣味出现杂乱、花哨、艳俗的浮华特征，正是因为没有现代设计这个价值观的支撑造成的，如果有现代设计这个审美观念的支撑，即使是红火和花哨，也可以被转换成有民族特色的当代审美趣味。几乎所有艳俗艺术的作品的语言，都呈现出不同程度的艳丽、花哨和红火的特征。《艳妆生活》展中的杨卫、胡向东、刘峥、王庆松都使用了与农民喜庆有关的符号，诸如把萝卜、大白菜的丰收景象与流行文化符号的混置，通过滑稽的模仿达到反讽的效果。所有艳俗艺术，都不同程度地使用了滑稽模仿这个60年代观念艺术首创、但盛行至今的语言方式，如常徐功象JEEF KOONS那样直接雇用刺绣艺人，用艳丽、光亮的丝线来表现农民企业家。罗氏兄弟则直接把60—70年代的新年画一农民喜庆丰收的景象、年年有余、胖娃娃等喜庆形象，与消费形象一卡拉OK机、可口可乐等直接拼贴混置，并用他们擅长的传统漆画工艺，使画面更加平滑、光亮、艳丽和滑稽。

俸振杰作品

王庆松作品

也许南方商业文化更盛，南方的艺术家多偏重对消费文化的反讽，语言方式更接近美国方式，广州《卡通一代》中的黄一瀚，多用流行的卡通玩具现成品和图片形象，或类似GILBERT GEORGE的画面，或类似美国走红艺术家CHRIS BURDEN把卡通玩具堆积一地的方式。四川的余极使用多媒体电脑的界面，制作了流光溢彩的鲜花和女人、艳丽多姿的感观世界等流行形象的大杂烩，“是对大消费生活状况的表面模拟，是光线夸张浓烈的布景舞台，同时作品也是一种浮华表象本身(摘自余极的创作手记)”。有些作品大量使用了廉价的“金灿灿”的材料，如孙平的新作等。虽然这里没有明显的农民符号，但其廉价的艳丽，与暴发的红火趣味相一致，甚至我们从那些廉价的卡通玩具中，看到乡镇企业的痕迹。

当然，俗文化语境的巨大力量使俗艳艺术显得微不足道，这也给了艳俗艺术以挑战，使更有语言强度的作品和艺术家的出现成为可能。

1997·9

王庆松作品

王庆松作品

Parodying "Peasant Style Get-Rich-Quick Taste"

— A Second Commentary on Gaudy Art Discourse

★ Li Xianting

Since the two exhibition's "Life in Gaudy Dress" and "Model for the Masses" took place in the first half of 1996, artists involved in Gaudy Art strategies have been developing more mature work, demonstrating modes of discourse that are uniquely related to their intention. Artists such as Li Lu-ming and Sun Ping from Hunan, Yu Ji from Sichuan, Yuan Wenbin of Fujian and the self-styled "Cartoon Generation" art collective from Guangzhou,all concern themselves with trends toward gaudiness and rampant consumerism. Before the above exhibitions, much of their work had revealed a discoursethat seemed excessively uniform.

Nevertheless, that artists continue to beconcerned with gaudiness and consumer culture, serves to illustrate that Gaudy Art remains an area of focus in contemporary culture. Especially withthe language it employs. Gaudy Art is clearly influenced by the kitsch work of Jeff Koons, but in part this has been an inspiration for artists not to ignore the ubiquitous presence of such gaudy culture in present day China. The parodying nature of Gaudy Art is not an attempt to cater to the tastes of the masses. Rather it demonstrates the powerlessness of art to impact on the pervasiveness of consumerism in today's reality. Whilst we may also currently advocate an intellectual role for artists it is not one of a return to produce Fine Arts in some ivory tower. Art is not able to change society anymore than art criticism is limited to one critical response, however, such discourse can provide a powerful framework for understanding visual arts. By maintaining an independent and often satirical point of view, artists can document the fact that we live in an age in which our lives are overrun by gaudy taste. What more powerful form of criticism of gaudy culture might we expect from today's artists? I am reminded of a story about Chen Duxiu (one of the founding fathers of China's Communist Party), who, in the early part of this century called for the destruction of scholarly painting and advocated instead what was then seen as "common" realism. Yet, when he saw that Shanghai Calendar Posters employed a form of realism which seemed to glamorize the new modern woman and the new modern lifestyle, Chen Duxiu reverted to the posture of those whose work he had initially held with disdain.

Popular culture has thrived, but only within certain limits. For example, Chinese New Year wood-block prints were only popular with the peasants in the countryside. The shift to popular culture as the mainstay of an entire society's aesthetic taste is a uniquely modern phenomenon. In fact, the popularization of culture was a process that emerged from the top - down. The subversion and eventual replacement of the scholarly tradition began in the late Qing Dynasty with Kang Youwei and Liang Qichao, and continued in the May Fourth period with Chen Duxiu, Qu Quibai, Lu Xun and others. They all took aim at the scholar tradition with the view that by doing so they could save and re-invigorate the nation. In keeping with their attempts at reaching out to the masses, they strongly advocated a popularization of the arts and targeted the refinemen of the scholarly tradition. This tradition had existed before the formation of modern China, and was a type of aristocratic culture that was part of the mainstay of the nation. On to which China's Scholar Gentry Culture - The Qin [stringed musical instrument], Chess, Calligraphy, Painting, Tea Gardens and the like belonged. These things formed the orthodox aesthetic taste of society and largely influenced popular culture.

Since the introduction of realist techniques into Chinese "Gongbi" style painting by Castiglioni at the end of the Qing Dynasty, Chinese art and for that matter Chinese lifestyles have generally cast aside scholarly culture and haute couture. As a result, almost every aspect of our lives today are permeated by popular culture. Good or bad, this is perhaps one of the most significant legacies the May Fourth Movement [begun in 1919]. (See my articles "A Criticism of the May Fourth 'Artistic Revolution'" and "An Overview of the Modes of Mao Zedong Art") As a leader of the Communist Party in 1943, Qu Qiubai personally led the Yanan art and literature movement aimed at popularizing the arts in Suzhou [a garden city where scholarly gentry culture thrived]. In the previous year, Mao Zedong had given his "Talk at the Yanan Roundtable Discussion", giving direction and impetus to the movement. He concluded that to learn from the peasants and their art was the only way to create a style of art that China's workers, peasants and soldiers would listen to and to observe. The art that came out of the fervor of the Yanan art and literature movement, included musical works such as "The Yellow River Chorus, " also Operas such as "The White Haired Girl, " and the wood-block prints of Gu Yuan that all derived from peasant art forms. Of course these were not the original forms of peasant art. Even so, as an aesthetic taste, peasant art had become the wellspring and model of inspiration and direction in art. Peasant art had replaced the scholar aesthetic. Not long after, with the arrival of commercial advertising came the creation of calendar poster art, with its origins in Western realism. As late as the Qing Dynasty, Chinese scholars had refused to accept either Western art or the tradition of Realism deeming both as "unrefined" (Zhang Puxin). It was for this reason, no doubt,

Castiglione eventually incorporated Chinese lines and even-lighting techniques into his art. Castiglione's infusing of Western techniques into a Chinese style also had an impact on Realist oil paintings produced in the late Qing . This form of "Trade Painting" downplayed the expressiveness of the brush stroke, which was central to both the Chinese and Western aesthetic at the time. And, perhaps largely for this reason, Realism and oil painting were relegated to the status of being popular art forms in China. Calendar poster art employed a technique based on watercolor mixed with a charcoal or carbon powder. Highly developed through slick, bright, pretty and celebratory art form techniques, these posters were usually associated with Chinese New Year celebrations. They quickly became a uniquely Chinese popular art form. Just before the New Year, they would be mass-produced and distributed mainly throughout urban areas. By 1949, however, the calendar posters had emerged in the farthest reaches of the countryside, eventually replacing the more traditional wood-block prints. In 1958, a number of writers conducted research into why calendar poster art eventually came to monopolize the market. They concluded that "the masses liked the rendering of 'bulging' noses and eyes [a reference to depth, not used in traditional wood-block prints] They liked styles that were "bright and clean." (Pu Songnian). " New Year's Paintings were hung not only for decorative purposes, but to bring good fortune." (Mao Zaisheng, see 1958, April and June issues of "Fine Art") In the early fifties, China organized a number of large-scale New Year's art movements. Several well-known oil painters and print artists participated. Chinese New Year's art at the time was known for "outline and shade," something in between print art and calendar poster art. At almost the same time, Dong Xiwen created his seminal "The Founding Ceremony of the New Nation" in the manner of New Year's art. In the succeeding years China accepted Soviet influences. Besides reflecting new life and serving the party, the emphasis was on developing the basic techniques of Realism, along with dramatic narrative. The impact was enormous. Narrative was something Chinese painting had cast aside since the Song Dynasty even if it had managed to persist in folk art traditions and especially in wood-block prints associated with New Year's celebrations. Traditional scholars viewed narrative as "a basic mode of life" and as such inherently common. Still, as much as it had an impact, the "pro-Soviet" camp of artists were dealt a serious blow with the anti-rightist campaign of 1957. The following year the nation again hoisted the flag of the Yanan tradition and the "national style." Even calendar poster art was rehabilitated as a legitimate art form. The same year, the entire staff of the Central Academy of Art's Preparatory School came together to create the oil painting entitled "Contemporary Hero", again in the manner of New Year's art.

The thread of popularization continued even through the "red, shiny and bright" art of the Cultural Revolution. The taste and aesthetic values of both calendar art, which came about to meet the needs of a [pre-revolution] consumer society, and the national style, which drew on peasant New Year's art to meet the needs of ideology, formed a confluence that eventually became a system of aesthetic values. There are three main reasons for this: Firstly , Mao Zedong accepted the Leninist principles that art is a cog in the Revolutionary Machine and that the Revolution was an important strategy for mobilizing the masses. Thus for the purposes of educating and uniting the people, it was only natural that art served the interests and tastes of workers, peasants and soldiers. It had to be what they liked to listen to and look at. And, in as much as the vast majority of the workers and soldiers were peasants, it was in fact to serve their own needs. Secondly, unlike Mao Zedong, most of the reigning leadership comprised of peasants. High and low culture were the same. Finally, as Lenin once said, " The triumph of the revolution is the people's holiday." Since seizing power, the Communist Party has been celebrating its own triumph, just like celebrating a holiday. And for China, the most important holiday of the year is the New Year which is celebrated with the most gusto by the peasants. Thus, red, shiny and bright; the celebratory style of New Year's paintings was born of the joy of "mankind's great victory", the joy which China reveled in at the same time as they were completely alienated and shut off from the rest of the world.

This kind of art and the displacement of former art forms were the result of the reality of the ideology of class struggle, that had at its core the dictatorship of the proletariat. The 1911 Revolution and the May Fourth movement both materially and philosophically reformulated scholarly gentry culture. After the victory of the Communist Party, the re-distribution of land, brought to an end the basis of such culture. The aristocracy, country gentlemen, old-styled scholars, even the newly emergent capitalist class and the nouveau riche were all brought down. And, the material basis for their lifestyle was completely and utterly destroyed. Following 1949, each successive political movement, ie. "Smash the Four Olds, Build the Four News", etc., further chipped away at the philosophical basis of the old culture, eventually bringing its demise. Furthermore with the ceasing of scholar gentry culture so went the philosophy and schools of thought developed during the May Fourth movement. Movements such as "Smash the Old, build the New"; "Destroy the capitalists, Rise up the proletariat"; "Backwards to bring down scholar gentry culture, forward to bring down capitalist culture" had disasterous consequences. In the end, all that was left was proletarian culture. And, the essence of proletarian culture was the above mentioned confluence of New Year's art and Calendar poster art - - a peasant culture created both by and for the national ideology.

The ruling classes comprised mostly of peasants naturally found forms of expression that suited the purposes of the Cultural Revolution - - we were surrounded by these fiery reds and popular forms which emerged in 1949 and lasted until the late 1970's. Even everyday things like a tea cup, a book bag or a bed sheet would be imprinted with the national banner, the red flag or a slogan. Except for this, at least from the standpoint of mainstream society, China has never created any other form of culture that could claim to be based on a unique system of values. Thus, since 1949, cultural movements have continued non-stop, trends have come and gone.

But, almost without exception, every trend has lived by and died with political change. Nonetheless, so pervasive was each successive trend that each spilled over into various aspects of the daily lives of the entire population. City planning in Beijing in the 1950's for instance resulted in the large-scale undertaking to remove large sections of the old city wall, along with vast numbers of old buildings. The purpose was to "smash the old world and build a new world." To be more specific, we can look at the changes undertaken in Tiananmen Square, The Daqing Gate and the Thousand Step Hall which had been removed. The original plan also called for the Forbidden City Palace to be partially cleared to enlarge the Square. This was to make room for the inspection of troop parades and mass rallies, more in the manner of the Soviet Union but also to meet the needs of political ideology. Not long after in the 1970's, many cities in China followed suit and built large Squares and Memorials. Even towns and villages erected Mao stat uesand walls inscribed with slogans. In the 1980's with the opening of China to the outside world, some leaders advocated high-rise buildings in the name of modernization, whilst other leaders insisted on topping the buildings with "hats" to emphasize the national character. Again, what took place in Beijing in the days and months to follow quickly spread throughout the rest of the country . When Beijing builds a few glass buildings, before long, the same thing can be seen emerging in other cities of China. If tiled walls are the craze in Beijing today, tomorrow you can bet they'll be covering the walls of buildings large and small throughout China. There is not a single city in which you can see more than the traces and threads of its architectural heritage, history and culture. What you have instead are the imprints of different ideologies, alongside hideously vulgar houses and streets devoid completely of cultural values.

That many of the last vestiges of past architectural forms are slated for demolition to make room for new construction is a reality that goes without saying. Perhaps just as disturbing are the buildings going up in their place. They are outfitted with "boots and hats", or some equally vulgar and superficial symbols of traditional culture. As for modern architecture, there is not much in the way of innovative form or detail to see. We do not have the research in modern art and architecture. Neither do we have its materials, its values, or for that matter any of those things upon which modern buildings must rest. This is because we oppose modern art, its aesthetics and values. We want national characteristics, yet we destroy our living heritage; We want modernization, yet we reject modern aesthetics and concepts.

Since the beginning of the eighties, the revolutionaries values instilled in the hearts and minds of the population over the course of several decades, fell out of favor. In the remaining vacuum, Taiwanese and Hong Kong's pop culture rushed in. Singers and movie stars replaced revolutionary heroes and became the new idols of today's youth. In fact, with the introduction of Western Fine Arts, Culture and Consumerism - videos compact-discs, fashion, pop songs, fast food, etc., whether they were items in daily use or food products, there wasn't any part of our lives that hadn't been permeated with either the look or sound of such things. Before Fine Art and culture could gasp its first breath of air in China, the early 1990's brought unprecedented economic prosperity. With it emerged the showy ostentatiousness that grew out of Western consumer culture and the multi-colored peasant dreams of hitting it big and, getting rich. Henceforward, the gods of wealth, so long suppressed, were invited back: Slogans like "Wealth, Rank, Longevity and Happiness", "Honor and Wealth", "Overflowing Springs of Wealth", 8888 [the number eight sounded phonetically like the word for "get rich"] were to be found everywhere. With economic prosperity, these spirits returned from the dead.

Red, the celebratory color of the peasantry, having completed its historical mission in service of the Revolution, once again plastered the walls. Big red lanterns replaced the red flag; Red advertisements took the place of yesterday's red character posters; Neon lights, an aphrodisiac of Western consumerism swept across the night sky of China. They were multi-colored, but mostly red and, always flashing.This taste is also reflected in our daily use, items such as furniture, clothing, even architecture. It seems that no matter where we go or what we look at, we cannot escape this flashiness and especially the color red. Even electronic products, something almost exclusively foreign, are decorated with bright colors and flashing lights. You smile because you're too embarrassed to cry. The fiery gaudy colors and flashiness of this culture is what I refer to as peasant-like, get-rich-quick taste. To "get-rich-quick" (literally "baofa") means to explode as might a firecracker, originally connoted the celebratory nature of fireworks and bright colors associated with holidays. Today, however, the expression is almost devoid of its original meaning, representing anything but the plainness and simplicity of peasant culture. That the "get-rich-quick" taste kept as its trademark the color red only serves to illustrate my point, that today's aesthetic values are more a matter of convenience and utilitarianism than any system of aesthetic values. Red began as something employed by national ideology for political purposes. It was then adopted by consumer culture for advertising and sales purposes. In as much as it is not the product of either a traditional or modern system of aesthetic values, it exists only as a kind of spontaneous, practical and ostentatious sign of the times.

Modern design is an important part of any modern society's aesthetic culture and values. It normally reflects the values of society albeit with elements of that society's Fine Arts. With this in mind, now consider the ostentiatiousness, flashiness and clutter of everything from neon signs to daily goods packaging in today's China. It is precisely because these things were produced without modern design concepts and values that they are as they are. With the support of modern design aesthetic values, even flashy reds might be transformed into something reflecting national character and values.

In the language of almost all Gaudy Art works appears the characteristics of garishness, flashiness and the color red. The artists Yang Wei, Hu Xiangdong, Liu Zheng and Wang Qingsong who exhibited in "Life in Gaudy Dress" employ symbols related to peasant celebrations, such as large harvests of turnips and cabbages which might be mixed symbols of pop culture, incorporating satirical copying to achieve the effect of parody. All Gaudy Art, to some extent employs the satirical parody attributed to post-modernism. However, the mode of discourse that has persisted until the present as seen in the works of Chang Xugong resembles more the work of Jeff Koons. Like Koons, Chang employed workers to produce his art, which in Chang's case were flashy, brightly colored silk-embroidered portraits of peasant entrepreneurs. The Luo Brothers employ New Year's paintings popular in the 60's and 70's in their lacquer works. Images of peasant's celebrating the harvest, chubby babies and motifs of abundance were cut and pasted alongside consumer images of Karoake Machines, and corporate logos, Coca-Cola, etc. then lacquered onto wood. Their works are flat, glossy, brightly colored and satirical.

Due to the fact that commercial culture is more thriving in the South, there is an emphasis solely on parodying consumerism. The mode of discourse is closer to American artists. For instance, Huang Yihan often uses cartoon toys and images directly in his work. The works of this group are also reminiscent of England's living sculptors Gilbert and George or American artist Chris Burden with his affinity with taxonomies of stuffed animals. Sichuan artist Yu Ji uses the world of multi-media computer art to produce glossy, colorful flowers and women in various shapes, sizes and perspectives in a riot of popular images. "On the surface, these are imitations of consumer life, like real-life stages with backdrops of exaggerated lines and color. At the same time, they are the very image of ostentatiousness." (Excerpted from the artists notes on his works) Some artist's works employ lots of cheap, gold-glitter materials, such as the works of Sun Ping, even if peasant symbols are not immediately apparent in his works. Still the cheap flashiness of his materials and the get-rich-quick symbolic of the color red are consistent. To the extent that these works also employ cheaply made cartoon toys, we can see the traces of the rural enterprises that specialize in such things. Of course, the overwhelming power of the language of vulgar culture makes Gaudy Art seem almost insignificant by comparison. Still, herein lies the possibility that such a challenge will result in stronger, more powerful forms of artistic language.

1997.9

平民时代的“贵族”布景

——“艳俗”的文化品位和艺术品质

★ 廖 雯

“艳俗”所指证的是90年代中期以来中国文化的基本特征，这种特征充盈着我们整个的生存环境和意识空间。我们周遭的一切，无不是各种文化传统尤其是“贵族”文化传统的粗制滥造的模仿和仓促临时的拼凑，不分功能、不分场合、不分时空、不分古今中外……由于失去了贵族的时代精神作为阅读和理解的基本前提，这种挪用和模仿只是一些文化外壳和碎片。仿佛匆忙布置起来的一个大舞台，人人争当“贵族”的好戏就这样上演起来。在这种急功近利的“扮演”中，人们忽略了最重要的一点：我们失落的不仅是贵族的身份，而是整个的贵族时代。那些匆忙建造的模仿碎片，只是一种无望实现的贵族梦想的布景。值得注意的是，相对于中国长期以来形成的、一时不能彻底改变的物质和精神的贫困状况中国古代、西方古代的贵族传统，西方现代的商业文明，乃至明星生活等，在人们心目中几乎都具有“贵族”意味。

贵族时代与平民时代

在本世纪之前，人类在贵族时代生活了两千多年。这个以严格的等级制维系的家族式的大厦，除了极少数这个家族的成员——贵族作为统治者拥有不劳而获的特权外，其他的人都是为此服务的被统治者。这个时代已经被上世纪末开始的全人类的革命彻底颠覆了。这个以充裕的人力、物力、时间供少数人享乐，从而充分体现了这个时代高贵典雅、雍容华贵、精雕细刻等特征的贵族文化，理应封存为人类历史某一阶段的辉煌的文化记忆，统统放进博物馆供人们瞻仰。犹如恐龙失去了远古的存活环境成为化石，逝去时代的“文化”，由于丧失了其生存和发展的时代精神和社会语境，保存下来的文化样式，对当下时代只具有“文物”价值而不具有“文化”意义。而我们的时代是一个以等价交换为原则的平民时代，自由作为这个时代最基本等价交换，不仅是商品经济的流通尺度，同样也是人际关系的平等准则。所有的人必须以自己的才智、时间和精力创造财富，与他人同样以自己的才智、时间和精力创造财富进行交换，这使竞争有了必备的起跑线。因此，这个时代的精神是人人进取，而不是荣华富贵。也正是有了这种历史在进取层面上的充分化作为社会基础，文化生存圈、艺术氛围、知识分子群体才有了产生和发展的可能。我们上世纪末本世纪初的全人类的革命，不正是为了建立这样共同创造、共同享受的大众时代而奋斗的吗？

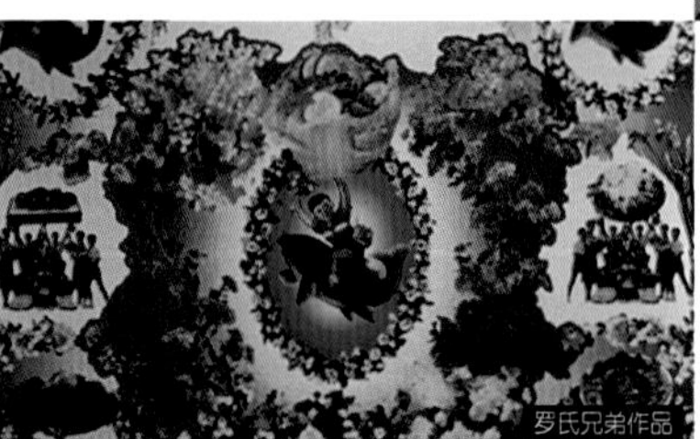
罗氏兄弟作品

王庆松作品

遗憾的是，我们的当下文化不是建筑在这样的时代精神上，而是一边疯狂地将各种传统文化已臻完美的样式打成碎片，号称“不破不立”；一边又生吞活剥地对这些碎片做表层的模仿和拼凑，以为“弘扬民族文化”，且颇引以为荣、引以为乐，而以此获得社会知名度乃至高官厚禄的人也不胜枚举。如果说普通百姓在生活中模仿“贵族”、“明星”效果，是失于全民物质状况和文化素质的普遍贫乏，那些以这“家”那“师”自居的“文化人”呢？他们在“弘扬传统文化”的旗帜下都做了些什么呢？给抄袭的西方现代建筑样式局部，戴上中国皇宫王府的琉璃瓦大屋顶？把朴素的青砖灰瓦民居，都安上玻璃门和雕梁画栋？在亮晶晶的迪斯科舞厅刺眼的霓虹灯中，装

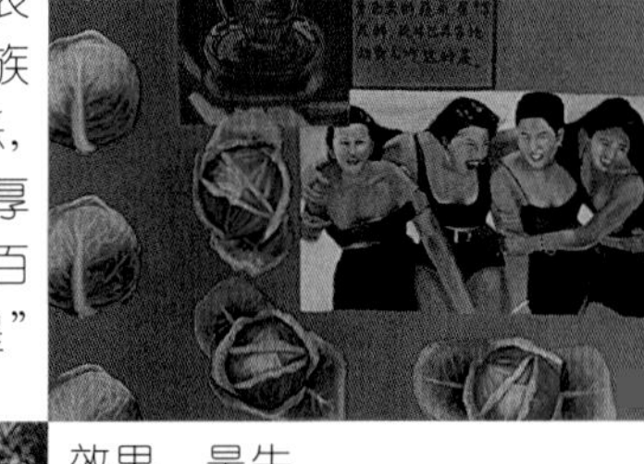

罗氏兄弟作品

李路明作品

配上一两件石膏的或塑料的仿罗马雕像？把追求淡泊超远、写意神似作为最高境界的文人画，涂上阴影透视去粉饰太平？把修身养性的书法弄成到处可以表演的杂耍？……传统文化正是在这一片“弘扬”声中被残酷地践踏了。我每每看到想到这些，心中充满悲哀和愤怒！这种无知而又自以为是、贫乏而又虚荣的社会心态，是从上至下的，也是90年代中国“艳俗”产生的基本语境。

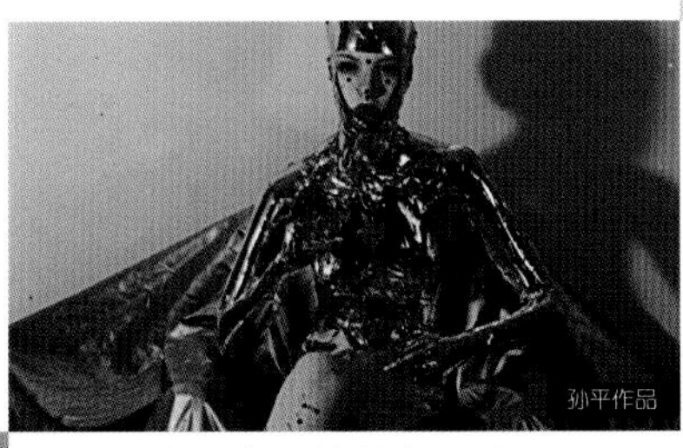
孙平作品

刘峥作品

因此，“艳俗”所标志的文化特征，不仅是一种文化样式，更标志着一种社会观念、心态、趣味和行为方式。在这点上，我们走的路几乎与西方60—70年代相同。19世纪西方工商业的发展，迅速造就了一个新兴的中产阶级，而“生活得象个贵族”一时成为中产阶级的追求目标。他们模仿18世纪贵族的闲暇、奢侈的生活方式，从穿著打扮到情感表达，甚至不惜将女人重新当成私有财产封锁、闲置于家庭，以标志自己经济和政治地位的上升。同样，由于整个贵族时代的失落，这种追求的结果，不可能是贵族文化的死灰复燃，而导致了另一种文化的产生，这种文化带有鲜明的这个时代的特征：炫耀财富的浮华、大众化的世俗、贵族文化样式的模仿的痕迹等。这种情形在60-70年代发展到了顶峰，即西方学者称为“媚俗”的一系列的文化样式、审美趣味以及行为方式，所不同的是，中国长期以来物质的匮乏、文化的贫瘠和目前追赶现代化时间的仓促，使媚俗文化的品位更“俗”；半个世纪以来由官方主流文化倡导的向民间艺术的学习，使其媚俗艺术的品质更“艳”，且带有避免不了的意识形态意味。艳俗艺术的意义正是提示了这个文化针对点，尤其值得注意的是，我们的著眼点不仅是普通百姓，而更应是文化层面的媚俗心态、趣味和行为。

孙平作品

艳俗艺术与波普艺术

众所周知，90年代中期以前，波普艺术在中国当代艺坛颇为流行，至今余波未泯。如果我们说艳俗艺术是继波普艺术之后的又一新的艺术现象，那么艳俗艺术必定有其不同于波普艺术的文化针对点和艺术定位。

艳俗艺术与波普艺术同是大众文化的产物，因此，在语言方式尤其符号使用上都有许多共同的倾向，而在深层的意义指向上却有着本质的区别。我认为，波普艺术是以大众文化的形式和手段表现和歌颂平民时代典型的大众文化，以消解贵族文化的高高在上的“尊严”。如安迪·沃霍（AndyWarhol）的作品从选择的流行文化的语符影星梦露、可口可乐，到使用的方式转印、拼贴、并置，奥登伯格（ClaesOldenburg）的巨大而软得可笑甚至有点色情的巨大的工业产品，无不都是大众时代的产物，而这些产物正是以其赤裸裸的世俗化和铺天盖地的气势、速度，将以往贵族文化的尊贵、荣耀和精雕细刻淹没和荡涤的。中国的90年代初期的“政治波普”之所以有影响力，正是因为准确地把握了西方迅速涌进的大众文化，对以往中国最具“尊严”的意识形态的消解这一文化针对点。如王广义作品中西方名牌商业产品与文革时期大批判招贴的并置，余有涵以民间艺术方式对毛泽东形象的修改，冯梦波的电脑戏中扔可口可乐罐的可爱的红军、样板戏人物和以接见红卫兵的手势打“面的”的毛泽东等。波普艺术由于对流行文化样式和手段的借用而在语言方式上也都带有简洁、鲜明、扩张等广告化倾向，而对大众文化持积极态度。

于伯公作品

刘力国作品

艳俗艺术则具有明显的讽刺和批判意味，但艳俗艺术批判的不是大众文化的通俗和世俗，而是贵族向平民时代过渡时期心理偏差导致的无思想的文化现象。由于现实中的"艳俗"现象往往带有对贵族文化碎片的模仿痕迹，而艳俗艺术对此种现象夸张和过分模仿的语言方式，在一定程度上是对模仿的模仿，因此，很有些戏剧化。如辛迪·施尔曼（SindySherman）对60—70年代以来美国的各种媚俗情形的戏剧化模拟，颇似剧照，那些夸张的姿态、表情和化装、道具以及场景气氛，无不是经历过那个时代的美国人十分熟悉甚至体现过的；杰夫·孔斯（Jeffkoons）把两性关系夸张成演戏，而且是在遍地鲜花造就的过分的浪漫气氛中的当众表演，把西方人两性关系中矫揉造作的媚俗情绪、浮华虚假的媚俗趣味赤裸裸地揭示于光天化日之下，令自以为浪漫多情、风流儒雅的西方人无地自容。

中国继90年代波普艺术盛行之后，艳俗艺术近年来也逐渐成为又一个文化热点。1996年4—5月，我与栗宪庭共同策划的《大众样板》，杨卫等艺术家联合举办的《艳妆生活》，俸振杰的《皮肤的感觉》，罗氏兄弟的《浮华的伤害》等展览，提示的问题都与"艳俗"有关，且画面形式也都呈现"艳"和"俗"的共同点。如徐一晖陶瓷的《红宝书》和《快餐盒》，直接使用已经艳俗化的工艺陶瓷制作方式，朵朵鲜艳、光亮、"浪漫"的瓷花，簇拥着革命时期流行的"红宝书"和改革时代流行的"快餐盒"，提示着中国流行趋势由政治化向商业化的转变；俸振杰取名为《幸福》的系列，以满街流行的模拟各种时代有钱人结婚样式、明星恩爱的神态、动作的"婚纱摄影"为摹本，过分夸张其俗艳特征：新人造作浮华的姿态滑稽变形，"幸福"无比的脸色红得发紫，画面一片晃眼的但俗不可耐的银黄艳粉翠绿大红，揭示出消费和时髦背后的媚俗心态；胡向东在当下流行的吃喝风与健美风之间，找到了一种微妙而幽默的内在联系，有钱无文化还自以为是、自以为乐的暴发感，即在汤汁欲滴的大菜、疙瘩疙瘩的肌肉与土里土气的黄瓜萝卜之间被暴露无遗；罗氏兄弟《欢迎世界名牌》系列，将中国各个时期的年画、宣传画和当下满街世界名牌广告繁复地拼在一起，揭示出当下中国被消费文化大肆侵入的事实；王庆松使用电脑技术将自我形象与各种明星甚至女明星接在一起，模拟"追星族"圆着各种明星梦；刘铮则在20—30年代流行的月份牌美女和当下流行的时髦女郎之间，找到了十分相似的消费特质：漂亮、浮华、无知、造作。

余权作品

艳俗艺术目前还颇有争议。如果我们排除由于非艺术立场的指责，从学术角度作一个自我反省的话，艳俗艺术的问题是明显的。由于意义指向和语言方式上没有形成独立的面目，有些作品在不同程度上与现实的艳俗现象拉不开距离，与波普拉不开距离，与西方的艳俗艺术拉不开距离。这些在探索中的不成熟现象十分正常。艳俗艺术语言方式也许还需要经过实践日趋完善，但它无疑是90年代中期以来中国艺术一个新的文化针对点。

1997年5月

The "Noble" Composition of the Generation of the Common People

——The Culture Character and the Art Quality of "Kitsch"

★ Liao Wen

"Kitsch" is the basic characteristic of Chinese culture since the middle of the 90s. This characteristic fills the entire living environment and ideological space. Every thing around us is nothing else but all kinds of culture tradition, especially the rough copying . It is a rush of the "noble"culture tradition which doesn't not recognize functions, situations, time and space, today and ancient,foreign and native…… As it lost the generation spirit of the noble which is the premise of reading and copying are only some cultural shell or pieces. It seems a big stage being set up in a hurry and a good play being performed in which everyone is eager to be the "noble".

In this "performence"of eagering for quick success and instant benefit, people get the most important point—they miss not only their noble status, but also the whole noble generation. Those copy pieces being built with a rush are just compositions of noble dreams which can never be realized. It is worth to be noticed that the following things are of some "noble"meaning: the poor condition of material and mental life shaped in long time which can not be changed in a short time, the noble tradition from ancient China and ancient west, commercial civilization of the modern west, and the lives of stars.

杨卫作品

The Noble Generation and the Common People Generation

Before this century, man had been living in the noble generation for two thousand years. In this mansion which was maintained by the strict class system, the noble had the privilege to do nothing and to get almost everything, the rest people were ruled by this system. This generation has been overthrown by the mankind revolution started at the end of last century. The characteristic noble had plenty of manpower, material and time for the enjoyment of a small group of people, So that it fully refl ected that time's character of elegant, grace and working with great care. It should be kept as a brilliant cultural memory of a period of history of humanity, and be totally put into museums for people to pay a visit. Just as dinosaurs lost their living environment in remote antiquity and became fossils, the "culture" of the past time and the culture forms being preserved have only the value of "cultural relic"and without the meaning of "culture", they lost the generation spirit and social context in which they could live and develop.

Our time is a common people's time when we use the rule of exchanging of equal values. Being the basic exchange of equal values of this time,freedom is not only the circulation measurement of commodity economy but also the equal norm of relation ship among people. Everyone has to use his/her wisdom, time and energy to create wealth in order to exchange for other people's wealth created in the same way. And this helps to have a necessary equal footing for competition. The spirit of this generation is that everyone is keeping forging ahead and not having a fortune waiting there. Because there is such a historical progress as a social base, it is possible for cultural· subsisting circle, art atmosphere and intellectual groups to grow and develop. The mankind revolution at the end of last century and he beginning of this century was start just for such a mass generation in which people create and enjoy together. Isn't it?It is regretted that today's culture is not built on the spirit base of this generation. Instead, it on one hand insanely breaks the almost perfect troditional culture into pieces, saying "without destruction, without construction", and on the other hand it imitates and pieces together those culture pieces uncritically, considering " glorifing national culture". Someone takes this as glory, and someone takes this as happiness. It is too numerous to mention one by one those who use the above way to get the well-known status and high positions and

田力勇作品

田力勇作品

handsome salaries in our society. If the ordinary people copping the"noble"of"star"effect is due to their poor material and cultural qualities, how about those cultural people who have such titles as "specialists"or masters? What do they do under the flay of "glorifying national culture"? Are they lifting the parts of modern western architecture and putting the glazed tiles of Chinese imperial palace as the cover of the building? Are they arranging glass doors or carved beams and painted rafters for people's grey brick houses? Are they matching one or two gypsum or plastic statues imitating Rome to a sparkling disco dancing hall with dazzlingrneon? The highest level of cultural people's painting is seeking no fame and wealth as well as being alike in spirit. And are they trying to add some perspective on it to present a false picture of peace and prosperity? Are they changing the calligraphy which can help to cultivate one's moral character to be a variety show performed every where? ······ Traditional culture is being trodden in the voice of "glorifying". Each time I see these, my heart is full of sorrow and anger. The state of mind of considering oneself always in the right and vanity can be found from the top to the bottom of the society, but actually it comes from ignorance and poverty. This is the basic context from which "kitsch" was born in China in the 90s.

The culture features of "kitsch"is not just a culture pattern, but it more symbolizes a social concept, a mentality, an interest and a behaviour. From this point, our way is similar to the western way in their 60s to 70s. The development of industry and commerce of the west in 19th century created a new middle class rapidly. "Living as the noble"became the goal of the middle class which copied the living way of leisure and luxury enjoned by the noble of 18th century, from clothing to feeling expression. They even kept women as their private wealth again leaving them at home to show their rise in economy and politics. Because the noble time is gone forever, the seeking of old time can not make the dead noble culture glowing again. As a result, the struggle leads another culture produced. The new culturerhas clear features of common people: flash of showing off rich, common customs of the ordinary people and mark of copying the noble culture. This situation came to its peak between the 60s and the 70s and it was called "kitsch"by the western scholars which meant a series of cultural types, aesthetic standards as well as behavior.

The difference is that China has a long history of lacking of material and culture, and now we are in a hurry to catch up with the western modernization. These makes the "kitsch"culture even more kitsch. For the past half century the Chinese government has been guiding the main culture to learn from the folk art that makes the kitsch culture even move colourful and carries a lot of unavoidable meanings of ideology. The meaning of the colourful folk art is the announcement of this point. We should notice that our point in not on the side of the common people, but on the side of kitsch feeling, kitsch interest and kitsch behavior.

Gaudy Art and Pop Art

Everyone knows that before the middle of 90s pop art is very popular in Chinese current art circles and even today it still doesn't die out. If we say gaudy art is a NEW art appearing after pop art, gaudy art must have some fixed different cultural point and art position.

Gaudy art and pop art are both outcomes of common people's culture, they have similar tendency in many ways in using the language and other symbols, but their deep meanings are quite different in nature. I think that pop art using the form and means to the sings praises of common people's culture in the generation of the common people, in order to clear up the so called high"dignity"of the noble culture. Andy. Warhol chosesth popular language and symbol in his works, from film star to co ca-cola, as well as the shift printing, pieced together and put together. Claes. Oldenburg makes the huge sexy industrial product which is so soft that makes people laugh. They are all the outcomes of the generation of the common people and these outcomes flood and wash away the dignity, glory and working at something with great care of old day's noble culture, with the common customs without a stitch of clothing and the momentum blotting out the sky and cover up the earth. The Chinese "political pop"in the early 90s has its influence power just because it grasps the fast coming western common people's culture, and it clears up the cultural point of ideology which has the most dignity in China before. just as Wang Guang-yi combines the famous Chinese and western products with the big-character poster in the Cultural Revolution, Yu You-han changes the image of Mao Ze-dong by folk art, and Feng Meng-po creates the computer games in which beloved red army man throws the tin of co ca-cola and Mao Ze-dong stops a taxi with the same gesture when he reviewed the Red Guards. Pop art borrows the means of popular cultural form and its language has a simple, bright, expanding and advertising tendency. Pop art supports the common people's art positively.

Gaudy art obviously has sarcastic and critical meaning. However what it criticizes is not the popularity of the common people's culture, but the cultural phenomenon without ideological content which is brought about by the psychological bias in the transition from the noble class to the time of common people. As gaudy art phenomenon usually has the traces of noble culture pieces, and as it has too much exaggerating and imitating, it becomes a copy of the copy in some way and becomes rather dramatic. Sindy Sherman's dramatic imitations of various kitsch

affairs of 60s and 70s are like stage photos. Those exaggerated attitutes, expressions, make-ups, stage properties and stage atmosphere are exactly what Americans of that time were familiar with or experienced. Jeffkoons exaggerated the sexual relation as a drama and nakedly put it on to the audience in the sun, enabling the westerners, who thought themselves romantic and gentle, ashamed.

In China, after the popularity of the pop art in the 90s gaudy art is gradually becoming another cultural hot point. From April to May in 1996, exhibitions such as "Models from the Masses"planned by Li Xian-ting and me, "Gaudy Life" by Yang Wei and some other artists, "Recounting of skin"by Feng Zhen-jie, and" The Damage from the Flooding of China"by Luo brothers, are all concerned with "gaudy " and all the pictures have a common character which is gaudy.For example, Xu Yi-hui's "The Red Treasured Book"and "Fast Food Box"made by pottery and porcelain directly use gaudy art letting many bright and romantic flowers of porcelain to surround "the red book " of the cultural revolution and the "fast food box "of the reform period. They remind people that China is turning from politics to business, Feng Zhen Jie's series named "Happiness"takes the weddings of rich people in different times and stars' wedding photos as facsimiles to exaggerate their vulgarity. The couples's affected postures and funny changes are hard to accept, the faces are too red to show happiness, and the dazzling colours of silver, yellow, pink, green and red in poor taste show the vulgar tasters behind the modern. Hu Xiang-dong forms a kind of delicate and humorous link between the current fashion of eating and drinking and the fashion of vigorous and graceful activities.Some people consider themselves in the right, but they have money without having education. The feeling of becoming rich suddenly is exposed by dripping rich dishes, developed muscles, local cucumbers and radishes. Lo brothers' series named "Welcome the world's Famous Brand" announces the fact that China is being invaded greatly by consuming culture by putting together of New Year pictures of different times, propaganda pictures and the world's famous brand ads in almost every street. Wang Qing-song uses computer tedchnology to combine self image and all kinds of stars, even female stars, to copy the "following star group"to realize all kinds of star dreams. Liu Zheng finds out a similar character between the pretty ladies on the cover of the calendar of the 20s and 30s and the modern ladies today -- they are all pretty, showy ignorant and artificial.

栗宪庭 廖雯
Li Xianting Liao Wen

There is still debate on gaudy art now. The question of gaudy art is clear if we can get rid of the criticism not from art point, and if we can make a introspection focusing on art. Because the meaning and language have not become independent features,some works can not keep a distance in some degree with gaudy phenomenon in reality, with pop and with gaudy art in the west,it's quite normal to have such not mature phenomenon. The art language of gaudy art probably needs more practice to be perfect. But it is doubtless that gaudy art is a new cultural point of Chinese art in the middle of 90s.

1997.5

(Translater: Zhao Ding-sheng Proofing: Jeremy Goldkorn)

徐一晖 XU YIHUI

1964年　出生于江苏连云港市
1989年　毕业于南京艺术学院
展览
1999年　跨世纪彩虹—艳俗艺术　泰达当代艺术博物馆　天津
1998年　中国当代艺术展　雷蒙.莫班画廊　纽约
1998年　腐败分子　私人空间　北京
1997年　艺术收藏展　四合苑画廊　北京
1997年　里昂双年展　法国
1996年　大众样板　北京艺术博物馆　北京
1996年　现实：今天与明天—当代艺术展　国际艺苑美术馆　北京
1994年　第三回中国当代艺术文献展　华东师范大学　上海
1993年　后'89中新艺术展　香港艺术中心　香港
1989年　现代艺术大展　中国美术馆　北京
1987年　江苏现代艺术群众第一回展　南京艺术学院　南京
1985年　“江苏青年艺术周”现代艺术展　江苏省美术馆　南京

1964　Born in Liannyungang City, Jiangsu Province.
1989　Graduated from Nanjing Acaderny of art, now living in Beijing.
Exhibitions
1999　Ouh, La, La, Kitsch!　TEDA Contemporary Art Museum ,Tianjin
1997　Biennale de Lyon ,Lyon, France
1997　Exhibition of Collection ,CourtYard Gallery ,Beijing
1996　Reality . Today & Tomorrow-'96 Contemporary Art Auction, Holiday Inn Art Foundation
1996　Models From Masses ,Beijing Art Museum
1994　3rd China Contemporary Art Document ,Southeast Normal University, Shanghai
1993　Post '89-China New Art, Hong Kong Art Center
1989　China Modern Art Exhibition ,China Art Gallery ,Beijing
1987　First Jiangsu Modern Art Group ,Nanjing Academy of Arts
1985　Jiangsu Youth Art Week. Modern Art Show,Jiangsu Art Gallery, Nanjing

胡向东 HU XIANGDONG

1961年　出生于江苏
1988年　毕业于南京艺术学院
展览
1999年　跨世纪彩虹—艳俗艺术　泰达当代艺术博物馆　天津
1999年　当代中国艺术展　苏黎士　瑞士
1999年　“酚苯乙稀”塑料艺术展　北京
1999年　九九开启通道—东宇美术馆首届收藏展　东宇美术馆　沈阳
1998年　两性平台　泰达当代艺术博物馆　天津
1996年　“艳妆生活”专题展　北京
1996年　现实：今天明天—中国当代艺术展　北京

1961　Born in Jiangsu
1988　Graduated from Nanjing Academy of Fine Arts
Exhibitions
1999　Ouh, La, La, Kitsch! TEDA Contemporary Art Museum ,Tianjin
1999　Contemporary Chinese Art Switzerland
1998　Personal Touch, TEDA Contemporary Art Museum, Tianjin
1996　Gaudy Life, Beijing
1996　Reality-Today & Tomorrow—China's Contemporary Art

俸 振杰
FENG ZHENJIE

1968年 出生于四川
1992年 毕业于四川美术学院美术教育系，获学士学位
1995年 毕业于四川美术学院油画系，获硕士学位
现任北京教育学院美术系讲师，油画教研室主任
展览
1999年 跨世纪彩虹—艳俗艺术 泰达当代艺术博物馆 天津
1999年 中国性格：思想食品 埃恩霍温 荷兰
1999年 九九开启通道—东宇美术馆首届收藏展 东宇美术馆 沈阳
1999年 当代中国艺术展 苏黎士 瑞士
1998年 北京青年油画家邀请展 国际艺苑美术馆 北京
1998年 两性平台艺术展 泰达当代艺术博物馆 天津
1996年 皮肤的叙述 个展 首都师范大学美术博物馆 北京
1995年 第三届中国油画年展 中国美术馆 北京
1994年 中港台大专美术作品展 香港中文大学 香港
1994年 第二届中国油画展 中国美术馆 北京
1992年 今日状态.1992艺术展 四川美术学院美术博物馆 重庆
1992年 中国当代艺术研究文献展 广州美术学院图书馆 广州

1968 Born in Sichuan Province, China.
1992 Graduated from Fine Arts Education Dept of Sichuan Academy of Fine Arts
1995 Graduated from Oil Painting Dept. of Sichuan Academy of Fine Arts with MFA
Now teaching at Fine Arts Dept. of Bejing Institute of Education
Exhibitions
1999 Ouh, La, La, Kitsch ! TEDA Contemporary Art Museum, Tianjin
1999 Chinese Characters : Food for Thought,De Wette Dame , Eindhoven,The Netherlands
1999 Open Channels,Dong Yu Museum of Fine Arts,Shenyang
1999 Contemporary Chinese, Art Zurich, Switzerland
1998 The Academic Exhibition of Beijing Youth Oil Painters, Art Gallery of Beijing International Art Palace ,Beijing
1998 Personal Touch, TEDA Contemporary Art Museum ,Tianjin
1996 Recounting of Skin, Art Museum of Capital Normal University, Beiing
1995 The 3rd Annual Exhibition of Chinese Oil Painting, National Museum of Fine Arts ,Beijing
1994 The 2nd Chinese Oil Painting Exhibition, National Museum of Fine Arts ,Beijing
1994 Works by Fine Arts Students in Mainland China.Taiwan and Hong Kong, The Chinese University of Hong Kong
1992 Present State · 1992 Art Exhibition,Art Museum of Sichuan Academyof Fine Arts ,Chongqing
1992 Modern Chinese Art Research Documents Exhibition, Library of Guang zhou Academy of Fine Arts ,Guangzhou

1966年 出生于湖北
1991年 毕业于四川美术学院油画系
展览
1999年 跨世纪彩虹—艳俗艺术 泰达当代艺术博物馆 天津
1999年 中国当代艺术展 旧金山 美国
1999年 48届威尼斯双年展 意大利
1998年 台北双年展 台北市立美术馆 台北
1997年 王庆松油画作品展 伦敦
1996年 中国！波恩现代艺术博物馆 德国
1994年 第三回中国当代艺术文献展 上海

1966 Born in Hubei CHINA
1991 Academy of Fine Arts of Sichuan
Exhibitions
1999 Ouh, La, La, Kitsch! TEDA Contemporary Art Museum,Tianjin
1999 The 48th Venice Biennale, Italy
1999 China'S Contemporarg Art 1999,San.U.S.A
1998 Bienale of Taipei. City Museum of Art. Taipei
1997 Wang Qingsong Oil Painting Exhibition, London.
1996 Gaudy life, Beijing.
1994 The 3rd China Contempor ary Art Documenta, Shanghai.

王 庆松
WANG QINGSONG

罗氏兄弟 LUO BROTHERS

罗氏兄弟
罗卫东 瑶族 1963年生于广西南宁 87年毕业于广西艺术学院
罗卫国 瑶族 1964年生于广西南宁 87年毕业于广州美术学院
罗卫兵 瑶族 1972年生于广西南宁 97年毕业于中央工艺美术学院
1986年兄弟三人开始合作 现居住于北京 职业画家

展览
1999年 跨世纪彩虹—艳俗艺术 泰达当代艺术博物馆 天津
1999年 巴塞尔艺术博览会 瑞士
1999年 福冈美术馆收藏展 福冈 日本
1999年 旧金山现代美术馆收藏展 旧金山 美国
1999年 罗氏兄弟漆画展 艺术与公共画廊 日内瓦 瑞士
1999年 纽约时报千年展 纽约 美国
1998年 中国当代艺术展 雷蒙.蒙班画廊 纽约
1998年 中国当代艺术展 精艺轩画廊 温哥华 加拿大
1998年 第24届圣保罗国际艺术双年展“航线”部分 巴西
1998年 两性平台艺术展 泰达当代艺术博物馆 天津
1996年 浮华的伤害 个展 北京艺术博物馆 北京

LUO BROTHERS
Luo Weidong Born in Guangxi Zhuang Automo mous Region in 1963 and graduated from Guangxi Art College
Luo Weiguo Born in Guangxi Zhuang Artonomous Region in 1964 and graduated from Guangzhou Academy of Fine Arts in 1987.
Luo Weibing Born in Guangxi zhuang Autonomous Region in 1972 and graduated from College
Exhibitions
1999 Ouh, La, La, Kitsch! TEDA Contemporary Art Museum Tianjin
1999 Basel Art Exposition, Basel, Switerland
1999 New York Times Millennium Exhibition, New York,U.S.A.
1999 The Luo Brothers Lacquer Paintings, Geneve, Swifzer land.
1999 San Francisco Modern Art Museum Collection Exhibition,U.S.A.
1999 Fukuoka Art Museum Collection Exhibition, Fukuoka, Japan
1998 Persond Touch, TEDA Contemporary Art Museum, Tian Jin
1998 24th Saopauio Lnternational Art Biennale, Section "Navigation Line Brazil"
1998 San Francisco Art Exposition
1998 China's Contemporary Art, Vancouver, Canada
1998 China's Contempotary Art, Lehmann Ma very Gallery, NewYork
1997 Gaudy-ism Upsurge
1996 Injury of Ostentation, Beijing.

1972年 出生于河北
1992年 毕业于河北师范学院
展览
1999年 跨世纪彩虹—艳俗艺术 泰达当代艺术博物馆 天津
1999年 当代中国艺术展 苏黎士 瑞士
1998年 偏执 北京
1996年 艳妆生活 北京
1994年 第三届当代中国艺术文献资料巡回展 上海

1972 Born in Hebei
1992 Graduated from Hebei Normal College
Exhibitions
1999 Ouh, La, La, Kitsch ! TEDA Contemporary Art Museum,Tianjin
1999 Contemporary Chinese Art, Zurich, Switzerland
1998 Corruptionists, Beijing
1996 Gaudy Life, Beijing
1994 3rd China Contemporary Art Documenta, Shanghai

刘峥 LIU ZHENG

卢昊 LU HAO

1969 Born Beijing
1992 Graduated from Central Academg of Fine Arts.
Exhitiions
1999 Ouh, La, La, Kitsch! TEDA Contemporary Art Museum,Tianjin
1999 The 48th Venice Biennale, Italy
1998 Corruptionists,Beijing
1996 Solo Exhibition, WAN FENG Gallery Beijing
1995 Solo Exhibition, Art Gallery of Beijing Interational Art Palace
1994 Solo Exhibition, Art Gallery of Beiing International Art Palace
1994 Solo Exhibition, Sepctember Gallery Beijing

1969年 出生于北京
1992年 毕业于中央美术学院
展览
1999年 跨世纪彩虹一艳俗艺术 泰达当代艺术博物馆 天津
1999年 “酚苯乙稀”塑料艺术展 北京
1999年 48届威尼斯双年展 意大利
1998年 偏执 北京
1996年 个展 云峰画廊 北京
1996年 个展 罗马意大利
1995年 个展 国际艺苑美术馆 北京
1994年 个展国际艺术苑美术馆 北京
1994年 个展 九月画廊 北京

1963年 出生于山东济南
1989年 毕业于北京中央美术学院版画系
任教于北京广播学院、新闻传播学院
展览
1999年 跨世纪彩虹一艳俗艺术 泰达当代艺术博物馆 天津
1996年 现实：今天与明天一当代艺术展 北京
1992年 首届九十年代艺术双年展 广州
1992年 中国前卫艺术展 柏林 德国

1963 Born in Jinan City of Shandong Province
1989 Graduated from Etching Dept. Of Centre Academy of Fine Arts
Now a lecturer of Journalism & Communition College of Beijing Broadcasting Institute
Exhibitions
1999 Ouh, La, La, Kitsch ! TEDA Contemporary Art Museum(Tianjin)
1996 Reality-Today & Tomorrow—China's Contemporary Art
1992 1st China's Contemporary Oil Art Bienniale, Guangzhou
1992 China's Vanguard Art, Berlin, Germany

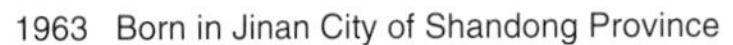

张亚杰 ZHANG YAJIE

邵振鹏
SHAO ZHENPENG

1961年 出生于青海西宁
1982年 毕业于青海师范大学（油画专业）
1987年 毕业于中央美术学院油画系助教班现为职业画家
展览
1999年 跨世纪彩虹—艳俗艺术 泰达当代艺术博物馆 天津
1999年 当代中国艺术展 苏黎士 瑞士
1996年 中国现代艺术展—现实：今天与明天 北京
1996年 邵振鹏油画展 TAO画廊 北京
1994年 中国前卫绘画大展 香港文化中心 香港
1992年 九十年代现代艺术展 北京大学 北京
1991年 中国民族艺术展 北京中国报社画廊 北京
1987年 首届中国油画展 上海美术馆 上海
1984年 第六届全国美展 辽宁美术馆 沈阳

1961 Born in Xining City. Qinghai Province, China
1982 Normal Univesity of Qinghai, Major in Oil Painting.
1987 Assistant Lector Class of the Oil painting Department, the Central Academy of Fine Arts, Beijing.
Exhibitions
1999 Ouh, La, La, Kitsch! TEDA Contemporary Art Museum,Tianjin
1999 The Exhibition of Comtemporary Chinese Arts, Zurichsee, Switserland
1996 Reality-Today & Tomorrow—China's Contemporary Art
1995 Exhibition of YuanMing Yuan Painters, Nanjing.
1994 The Painting Exhibition of Chinese Avant-guarde Artists,
1993 The Biennial Oil Painting Exhibition of China, National Art Museum, Beijing.
1992 Mordern Art Exhibition in 1990's, Beijing University.
1991 The Ethnic Art Exhibition of China, Beijing.
1987 The First Chinese Oil Painting Exhibition, Shanghai.
1984 The Sixth National Art Exhibition, Shenyang.

1962年 出生于北京
1989年 巴黎高等美术学院进修
1995年 法国高等造型艺术研究院
展览
1999年 跨世纪彩虹—艳俗艺术 泰达当代艺术博物馆 天津
1996年 “公寓／公寓”展 私人公寓 马赛
1995年 那普勒艺术基金会展 法国
1989年 中国现代艺术 中国美术馆展 北京
1988年 今日艺术 上海艺术画廊 上海
1987年 四青年油画展 中国美术馆 北京
1987年 中国油画展 上海美术馆 上海

1962 Born in Beijng
1987 Graduated from Centre Academy of Fine Arts
1991 Ecole Superieur de Beaux Arts , Paris
1995 L'institrt de Haute Elude eu Art Plastique
Exhibitions
1999 Ouh, La, La, Kitsch! TEDA Contemporary Art Museum,Tianjin
1996 Apartment/ Apartment, Private Apartment,Marseille, France
1995 Foundation Napoule, France
1989 Mordern Chinese Art, Museum of Fine Arts, Beijing
1988 Today's Arts, Shanghai Art Gallery, Shanghai
1987 Four Young Painters, Museum of Fine Arts in Shanghai,

尹齐
YIN QI

孙平
SUN PING

1953 Born in Guang Xi Province
1987 Graduated from Guangzhou Academy of Fine Arts
Exhibitions
1999 Ouh, La, La, Kitsch! TEDA Contemporary Art Museum,Tianjin
1998 North East AsiaContemparary Art Exhibition in Niigata, Japan.
1996 Reality:Present and Futre,Beijing
1993 China New Art Exhibition After 1989,Hong kong.
1992 The First 90s Biennial Art Exhibition,Guangzhou
1992 Chinese Game No1:Issuing RMB Stock A of Sunping Art Joint-stock Ltd. Operated Action Art in Guangzhou
1992 The Second Exhibition of Chinese Contemporary Art Researching Literature Reference ,Guangzhou

1953年 出生于广西
1987年 毕业于广州美术学院
展览
1999年 跨世纪彩虹一艳俗艺术 泰达当代艺术博物馆 天津
1998年 东北亚现代艺术展 日本新泻
1996年 '96东京.中国前卫艺术展 东京
1996年 现实：今天与明天一'96中国当代艺术展 北京
1993年 后'89中国新艺术展 香港
1992年 中国当代艺术研究文献资料第二回展 广州
1992年 中国游戏1号.发行中国孙平艺术股份有限公司人民币A股股票 行为艺术

李路明
LI LUMING

1956 Born in Hunan Praovince
1985 Graduated from the Postgraduate Department of the Chinese Art Research Institute and Won Master's Degree
Now a chief editor of the Overseas Modern Artist Translating Collection and Testing Art Collection.
Exhibitions
1999 Ouh, La, La, Kitsch! TEDA Contemporary Art Museum,Tianjin
1997 Metropolis Personality Combined Art Exhbition
1994 The Present Condition of the Chinese Contemporary Oil Painting Exhibition ,Hong Kong
1992 The First 90s Biennial Art Exhibition,Guangzhou
1992 The First international Art Fair in Asia,Hong Kong
1991 I Don't Play Cards with Cezanne—Chinese 80s avant- grade Art Exhibition,The American Asia Pacific Museum

1956年 出生于湖南
1985年 毕业于中国艺术研究院研究生部，获硕士学位
现为《实验艺术丛书》主编
展览
1999年 跨世纪彩虹一艳俗艺术 泰达当代艺术博物馆 天津
1997年 “都市人格，1997”艺术组合展 长沙
1994年 中国当代油画现状展 香港
1992年 亚洲首届国际艺术博览会 香港
1992年 首届90年代艺术双年展 广州
1992年 第二回中国当代艺术文献展 广州
1991年 新形象联展 长沙
1991年 我不与塞尚玩牌-中国90年代前卫艺术展
亚太博物馆 美国

赵勤 刘健
ZHAO QIN LIU JIAN

Zhao Qin
1967 Born in Xuzhou of Jiang Su Province
1989 Graduated from Art Department of Nanjing Art Institute
Exhibitions
1999 Ouh, La,La,Kitsch!TEDA Contemporary Art Museum,Tianjin
1998 "it's me",Beijing
1998 Corruptionists,Beijing
1997 China's Contemporary Art Invitational Exhibition,Hong Kong
1992 Contemporary Art Documents Exhibition,Guangzhou
1987 The first Chinese Oil Paiating Exhibition
1985 Modern Art Exhibition of "Jiang Su Youth art week"

Liu Jian
1969 Born in Yan Cheng of Jiang Su province
1993 Gradnated from art Department of Nan Jing Art Institute
Exhibitions
1999 Ouh, La,La,Kitsch!TEDA Contemporary Art Museum,Tianjin
1998 Corruptionist,Beijing
1998 "it's me",Beijing

赵勤
1967年 出生于江苏徐州
1989年 毕业于南京艺术学院美术系
展览
1999年 跨世纪彩虹—艳俗艺术 泰达当代艺术博物馆 天津
1998年 “it's me”作品展 北京
1998年 偏执 北京
1997年 中国当代艺术邀请展 香港
1992年 当代艺术文献展 广州
1987年 首届中国油画展 上海
1985年 “江苏青年艺术周”现代艺术展 南京

刘健
1969年 出生于江苏盐城
1993年 毕业于南京艺术学院美术系
展览
1999年 跨世纪彩虹—艳俗艺术 泰达当代艺术博物馆 天津
1998年 “it's me”作品展 北京
1998年 偏执 北京

于伯公
1970年 出生于内蒙古
1990年 毕业于黑龙江省工艺美校
展览
1999年 跨世纪彩虹—艳俗艺术 泰达当代艺术博物馆 天津
1998年 “生活样板”专题作品展 北京古老画廊
1998年 “现实的虚拟”开放的工作室展 北京慈云寺

1970 Born in Nei Mongolia
1990 Graduated at Heilongjiang Industrial Art School
Exhibitions
1999 Ouh, La,La,Kitsch!TEDA Contemporary Art Museum Tianjin
1998 Exhibition on a Special Topic:Life Model Gulao studio, Beijing
1998 From Rdality to AFiction—The Exhibition of the Open studio , Ciyunsi,Beijing

刘 力国
LIU LIGUO

1964年　出生于黑龙江省
1991年　毕业于中国戏曲学院舞台美术系毕业
展览
1999年　跨世纪彩虹—艳俗艺术　泰达当代艺术博物馆　天津
1996年　85-95年中国前卫艺术文献展
1993年　中国油画年展　北京
1989年　十人水墨画展　首都博物馆　北京
1986年　黑龙江省青年美术作品展　哈尔滨

1964 Born in Heilongjiang
1991 Graduted from Stage Design Department of Beijing Opera Institute
Exhibitions
1999 Ouh La,La ,Kitsch! TEDA Contemporary Art Museum,Tianjin
1996 85-95 China Contemporary Art Documenta
1993 China Oil Painting Exhibition
1989 Traditional Chinese Painting
1986 Heilongjiang Young Artist Exhibition

1953年　出生于台湾省彰化市
1979年　毕业于中国文化大学美术系
展览
1999年　跨世纪彩虹—艳俗艺术　泰达当代艺术博物馆　天津
1999年　台湾当代艺术系列-杨茂林个展　MOMA画廊　日本福冈
1999年　请众仙—文化父配大圆志　大未来画廊　台北
1998年　98立川国际艺术节　日本立川
1997年　第四届洛山矶国际艺术节—东方的灯笼　美国
1996年　台湾艺术主体性—认同与记忆　台北市立美艺术馆　台北
1995年　台湾当代艺术　澳洲雪梨当代美术馆　澳洲
1994年　开放纪元 巴西圣保罗国际双年展之台湾视角 台北汉雅轩
1991年　101杨茂林个展　台湾省立美术馆
1990年　Made in Taiwan-1台北市美术馆　台北
1987年　游戏行为　台北市美术馆　台北

1953 Born in Changhua,Taiwan
1979 Graduated from Fine Arts Dept.Chinese Cuiture Umiversity
Exhibitions
1999 Ouh, La,La,Kitsch!TEDA Contemporary Art Museum,Tianjin
1998 International Art FestivalTachikawa 1998,Japan
1999 Inviting the Immortals: Culture, Intercourse, Tayouan History, lin&Keng Gallery ,Taipei
1991 101Yang Mao-Lin one Man Show,Taiwan ProvincialFine Arts Museum
1990 Made in Taiwan-1,Taipei Fine Arts Museum
1987 Begavior of Game Playing,Taipei Fine Arts Museum
1997 Lantern of the East,1997-the 4th international Art Festival Los Angeles,La Artcore,Californls,USA
1996 Taipei Biennial:The Quest for Identity-Identity and Memories, Taipei Fine Arts Museum,Taipei
1995 Taiwanese Contemporary Art, Sideney Contemporary Art Museum Arstralia.
1994 The open era,Hanart Gallery Taipei
1994 Open Culture:The 22nd International Biennai of Sao Paulo from a Taiwan Prespectine Hanart Gallery

杨 茂林
YANG MAOLIN

顾 世勇 GU SHIYONG

1960 Born in Taichung County,Taiwan
1996 Doctoratd' Arts Plastiques de L'universite de Paris I(Pontheon Sorbonne).Received the highest honor "honorables avec felicitation"
1991 D.E.A d'Arts Plastiques de L'universite de Paris I
Diplome de l'Ecole Nationale Superieure des Arts Decoratifs de Paris
1990 Maitrise d'Arts Plastiques de L'universite de Paris Ⅷ
Currently an associate professor in the Department of AppliedAesthelics Fujen Catholic Universlly

Exhibitions
1999 Ouh, La,La, Kitsch! TEDA Contemporary Art Museum,Tianjin
1997 Villain and Hypocrite,IT Park Gallery
1994 Traveling Art Exhibition,Tung Chih Art Gallery
1994 History of Poetry in Taiwan-An Exhibition,Crown Gallery ,Taipei
1993 Paris Youth Art Gallery,Grand Palaice Paris
1993 Dark Bearing Series- Once,Taipei Municipai Fine Arts Museum Collection
1993 Black Whiriwind,A PU Art Gallery
1992 In the Clouds Causing Trouble,IT Park Gallery
1992 "Paris,Gap",Provincial Taichung Arts Museum
1988 Blue Wing,Taipei Municipai Fine Arts Museum Collection

1960年 出生于台湾省台中县
1990年 法国巴黎(圣丹尼)大学造形艺研所硕士
1991年 法国巴黎第一大学造形艺术研所 深造研究文凭
1996年 法国国立巴称第一大学艺术科学.造形艺术博士学位
现任教辅仁大学应用美术系副教授
展览
1999年 跨世纪彩虹—艳俗艺术 泰达当代艺术博物馆 天津
1997年 恶恶霸与天堂刀 伊通公园
1994年 游移美术馆 东芝画廊
1994年 台湾史诗大展 台北皇冠
1993年 黑旋风 阿普画廊
1993年 巴黎青年画展 巴黎大皇宫
1993年 台湾新风貌49-93'台北市立美术馆
1993年 台湾90'新观念族群,台北汉雅轩
1992年 飞宇、造次 伊通公园
1992年 巴黎·间距 省立台中美术馆

1968年 出生于台湾彰化县
1993年 文化大学美术系西画组毕业
1999年 国立台南艺术学院造形艺术研究所毕业
展览
1999年 跨世纪彩虹—艳俗艺术 泰达当代艺术博物馆 天津
1998年 进入华山 华山艺术特区 台北
1998年 新素描展 草土舍艺术中心 台北
1998年 化外之境 帝门艺术中心 台北
1998年 台湾艺术家联展 意大利米兰艺术学院 米兰
1998年 前卫艺术家过新年 诚品艺术空间 台北
1998年 艳俗台湾—生活是如此妆扮 大未来画廊 台北
1997年 逛天堂 新乐园艺术空间 台北
1996年 台北双年展 台湾艺术的主体性-权力与情欲
市立美术馆 台北
1996年 台北奖入选 台北市立美术馆 台北
1995年 SOCA成员联展 太平洋文化基金会 台北
1994年 台北县美展落进会外展 甜蜜蜜艺术空间 台北

1968 Born in Chuan-hua,Taiwan
1993 B A(Bachelor of Arts),Chinese Culture University,Taipei
1999 M.F. A(Master of Fine Arts) Graduate Institute of Plastic Arts Department ,Tainan National College of Arts

Exhibitions
1999 Ouh, La,La,Kitsch! TEDA Contemporary Art Museum,Tianjin
1998 Beyond the Substancial World,Dimension Art Center,Taipei, Taiwan
1998 Gaudy-ism Taiwan:Boorish& vuilgar As the Makeup of Life LIIN& kENG Gallery ,Taipei ,Taiwan
1998 Avant-Gqarde Artists Celebrate The New Year,Eslite Vision, Taipei Taiwan
1998 Artists Di Taiwan,Accacemia di Belle Arti Di Brera, Millano,Italy
1997 Barging into Heaven,Shin Leh Yuan(New Paradise)Art Space,Taipei,Taiwan
1996 Selected in Taipei Prize Taipei Fine Arts Museum,Taipei Taiwan
1995 SOCA workshop members,Taipei Taiwan
1994 Anti-Taipei County Art Exhibition,sweety Art Space,Taipei Taiwan

跨世纪彩虹——艳俗艺术

湖南美术出版社出版 · 发行
（长沙市人民中路103号）

编著：廖雯 栗宪庭
责任编辑：杨帆 刘昕
平面设计：俸振杰 高立仁

湖南省新华书店经销
北京嘉年正稿服务有限公司制版
深圳彩帝制版印刷有限公司印刷
开本:250x210毫米 1/16
印张：7
1999年5月 第1版
1999年5月 第1次印刷
印数：1-2000册

ISBN7-5356-1260-1/J · 1178
定价：88 元

阿静
洛阳哈斯曼
中国食品陈列柜市场占有率领先
专业乳品制造商
铸诚防盗门
APEX
星 艷
和大王
永和
24小时营业
堂雅文
拿浴
满江
太阳酒家
海鲜家常菜
中国
双星
SUN DONG AN PLAZA
朝内菜市场
堂雅文
家常菜
华鹤家具
华鹤木门
路华电器
龙丰集团
大石 保龄设备
大石 台球设备
北京金保康药业有限公司
BEIJING JINBAOKANG MEDICINE LTD. CO.
朝内菜市场
铜字牌匾
锦旗条幅
西饼蛋糕房
新添"面爱面"骨汤火锅
风格发廊
京金保康药业有限
JINBAOKANG MEDICINE LT